Note to Readers

While the Fisks and the Allertons are fictional characters, Levi and Katherine Coffin were Quakers who helped organize and run the Underground Railroad for decades. First in Newport, Indiana, and then in Cincinnati, they helped slaves escape from the South to freedom in Canada.

Because Cincinnati was just across the Ohio River from the South, it was an important stop in the Underground Railroad. The Coffins and their partners would hide slaves in secret rooms and move them safely on to the next stop in their travels. They provided disguises, food, and medical attention.

Before they reached Canada, most escaping slaves along this part of the Underground Railroad had been helped by other slaves, free blacks, whites, and Native Americans.

DANGER *on the* RAILROAD

Susan Martins Miller

BARBOUR
PUBLISHING, INC.
Uhrichsville, Ohio

ISBN 1-57748-259-X

Published by Barbour Publishing, Inc., P.O. Box 719, Uhrichsville, Ohio 44683
http://www.barbourbooks.com

Printed in the United States of America.

Cover illustration by Peter Pagano.
Inside illustrations by Adam Wallenta.

Chapter 1
Adventure at the Tracks

Even with her hands pressed hard against her ears, Christina Fisk could not block out the thunderous roar. She scrunched up her freckled face and squeezed her green eyes shut. The powerful blackened engine howled past her. Sparks spit off the steel wheels that pushed the mighty engine forward along the tracks. Tiny pebbles, helpless against the power of the engine, flew through the air. One of them dug into Tina's left cheek, causing her to cry out. But, of course, her cry could not be heard. The wind churned up by the train whipped her red hair into a tangled mass. But she dared not take her hands from her ears to control her hair or protect her eyes.

Tina opened one eye to the train. It was a freight train—a long one. In frustration, she took a few more steps back, even though she knew she could not get far enough away from the train to escape its roar. She was trapped. And it was all the fault of her brother Charles.

Still with only one eye open, Tina glanced over at Charles. At eleven years old, he was two years younger than Tina, but already taller than she was. She hated it when people thought he was the older of the two, which happened more and more often as he kept getting taller. But Tina was small, like her mother, and she knew she would never be bigger than Charles again.

Charles was saying something and pointing enthusiastically at passing freight cars. His voice faded away in the wind. Tina could not hear a word he said, but she tried to figure out what he was pointing at. Reading the lettering on the sides of the cars, she could see that the train was loaded with a variety of Cincinnati goods—everything from pork to shoes. This particular train was headed north.

No doubt Charles knew exactly what stops it would make and where its final destination would be. All he ever talked about was trains. Tina had to admit that she was impressed with how much he knew. But she did not understand why anyone would want to know that much about the railroad. She could never remember even a fraction of the facts Charles spouted off so easily.

At last the train passed, all fifty-six cars. Tina lowered her hands and let out her breath in relief.

"That was one of the best ones yet," Charles said. His brown eyes glowed in excitement under a mop of uncombed brown hair. He bounded over to the tracks and began walking between the rails in the dust of the train.

Reluctantly, Tina followed. "Do you really think it's safe to walk in the middle of the tracks?" she asked. Vainly, she tried to press her wild hair back into place.

Charles glanced over his shoulder at his sister. "The train is gone, Tina. I promise you, it is not going to back up and run us over."

Tina let her retort go unsaid. She was hot. The late September afternoon sun had made her tired. Tina was not sure why she had agreed to walk with Charles along the tracks west of town on a Saturday afternoon. Perhaps it was to get away from Daria and David, their four-year-old twin siblings. Daria and David could wear anyone out within half an hour, and they were louder than the rest of the family put together.

"We should have gone walking by the canals," Tina said. "It would have been cooler along the water."

"Aw, who wants to watch those poky old boats?" Charles responded. "A train can get a load of shoes from Cincinnati factories to Chicago stores in no time at all. The boats take forever."

"The people in Chicago can wait a few more days for their shoes," Tina insisted. "Before the railroad came through, everyone thought the canals were wonderful."

"Times change, Tina. This is 1854. The railroad did come through. Trains are more efficient."

Charles and Tina had had this debate more than once. Tina knew she could never persuade Charles of the peacefulness of the canals and the beauty of the Ohio River that flowed through Cincinnati. Yes, the river was pretty, he would agree. But the water could never compete with the power and speed of the railroad.

"Do you really think that train is going to Chicago?" Tina asked.

"Absolutely," Charles responded. "The CH&D goes north. There are a few transfer stations along the way. Then it meets up with the PFW&C, which goes west to Chicago."

"I wish you would quit talking in letters." Tina kicked at a loose rock.

"I've told you what the abbreviations mean," Charles said impatiently. "The CD&D is the Cincinnati, Hamilton, and Dayton line, and the PFW&C is the Pittsburgh, Fort Wayne, and Chicago line. It's very simple. The lines are all named after the places they go. I hope you at least remember what M&C means."

Tina thought for a moment. "Marietta and Cincinnati?" she offered hopefully.

Charles grinned. "There is hope for you after all."

Tina was relieved to have guessed correctly. She knew enough about Ohio geography to remember that Marietta was on the eastern side of the state, while Cincinnati was the major city on the western side. Surely there was a railroad that connected them, she had reasoned.

"Someday I'm going to go to Chicago," Charles announced. "It's an even bigger city than Cincinnati."

"But it's far away," Tina said.

Charles shrugged. "Don't you understand? With the railroad, you can go anywhere. It doesn't take weeks to get somewhere, like it does on the river. I could even live in Chicago and still visit Mama and Papa whenever I wanted to."

"I don't think I'd want to live anywhere else but Cincinnati," Tina said. "I like it here."

"I like it here, too," Charles said. "But this is not the only nice place in the country. Aren't you even curious about other places?"

Tina nodded. "I'd like to take a boat down the Mississippi, all the way to New Orleans."

"And then you could take the railroad back," Charles teased. "Someday the railroad will connect any two places in the country, even all the way out to the Pacific Ocean. You can't say that about your boats."

Tina stumbled over a railroad tie. Abandoning any ideas of ladylike behavior, she pulled her skirt up a few inches so she could see her feet. Her mother had insisted that at thirteen, Tina was old enough to wear her skirts well below her knees, but Tina found it inconvenient. A railroad bed was not exactly a smooth surface for an afternoon's walk in a long skirt.

"If I was going somewhere on a boat," Tina said, "I would not be in any hurry. There would be so many beautiful things to see along the way."

"Not everything would be beautiful," Charles said. "A trip down the Mississippi would take you straight through the South."

"I've heard that the South is very pretty. They have wonderful magnolia trees."

"Come on, you know what I'm talking about," Charles said impatiently.

"I know," Tina murmured. "Slaves."

"I'm not sure Mama and Papa would want you to take a trip through the South."

"I wouldn't buy a slave just because I went to New Orleans."

"Everyone along the way would expect you to have one, especially if you didn't travel with a servant."

"I don't need a servant. I can take care of myself."

Charles chuckled. "If Uncle Tim heard you were going south, he would give you an abolitionist errand to do."

Tina and Charles had grown up listening to Uncle Tim, their mother's older brother. He was very outspoken. Everyone in Cincinnati knew his opinion of slavery—that it was an immoral practice that degraded the value of human life. As a lawyer, Uncle Tim was doing everything he could to get the laws changed so that slavery would be illegal everywhere in the nation.

Tina straightened her shoulders and spoke authoritatively. "I remember when Congress passed the Fugitive Slave Law of 1850. You were too young to know what was going on."

Charles elbowed his sister's shoulder. "I know about that law. The local authorities are supposed to help slave catchers find escaped slaves."

"Uncle Tim doesn't like that law," Tina said. "I think he causes problems on purpose so that the sheriff can't help the slave catchers."

"Uncle Tim might move to Kansas, you know," Charles said.

"I am sure that Aunt Dot does not want to move to

Kansas," Tina retorted. "And Uncle Tim would never go without her."

"But he would if he could. Kansas and Nebraska are supposed to vote and decide for themselves whether they want to have slavery or not. Uncle Tim wants to move to Kansas so he can vote against slavery."

Tina was silent for a moment. It did not seem to her that moving to Kansas to cast one vote in such a controversial issue would do much good.

"He would only have one vote," she said. "Can one person really make a difference?"

"Every vote counts. Every person matters. That's what Uncle Tim always says."

They walked along in silence after that. Tina had several friends at school whose parents concentrated on their jobs and family life. They worked long hours in the factories and shops of Cincinnati. What little time they had left, they spent with their children.

Her friends concentrated on their schoolwork and chores and sometimes looked in the shops for some new fabric or ribbon. They seemed content to live a pleasant, routine life in a lovely, growing city. Some of the families she knew had come from the South or had relatives across the Ohio River in Kentucky. Not everyone agreed that slavery was morally right, but they did not spend all their energy fighting it.

But at the Fisk household, politics was always the topic of conversation. Tina's father was a doctor, and people came and went from his clinic all day long. While he did not lecture all his patients about their political views, he left stacks of literature around where everyone who came in would see them—antislavery pamphlets or newspaper articles crying out against the expansion of slavery in new states. No one had any doubt that Dr. Kevin Fisk was opposed to slavery in any form.

And then there were the relatives. Ben Allerton was her mother's uncle. Ben was a carpenter who ran a furniture factory with his son Fred. Ben had firm opinions, but he minded his own business. Tim Allerton, Tina's uncle, of course, was a public figure. He was not ashamed to try to persuade people to take up his opinions and fight for the causes he thought were important.

"I'm getting hot," Tina said to Charles. She was tired of thinking about slavery and politics. What she wanted most was a tall, cool drink of water. "Let's go home."

Tina stopped in the middle of the tracks, waiting for Charles to agree that it was time to turn around and find their way through the streets of Cincinnati to the Fisk home.

"Come on, Charles."

Charles cocked his head to one side. "Do you hear that? Another train is coming. From the north, this time."

Tina immediately jumped off the railroad tie where she had stopped and vaulted several yards clear of the tracks. She waited for Charles to follow, but he didn't.

"Charles, come on," Tina urged. She could hear the train now, too. It was coming fast.

"Here she comes!" Charles said. The glow was back in his eyes. He stood in the middle of the tracks and watched as the train bore down on him. "Sounds like the PCCL&SL—

that's Pittsburgh, Columbus, Cincinnati, and St. Louis."

"Charles, get off the track!" Tina did not care where the train was coming from.

"It's a long one. I can tell. That engine is working hard."

"Charles!"

The train was in view now, coming around a slight bend. Smoke puffed from the engine's chimney as it tugged its heavy load.

"Ah ha!" Charles exclaimed. "I was right."

Out of instinct, Tina stepped even farther back from the track. Finally Charles began to scuffle backward over the side of the rail. He jumped to the opposite side of the tracks from Tina.

The train bore down. Its horn blasted furiously.

Although he was finally off the tracks, Charles still craned his neck out over the rails. "Don't you love it?" he shouted over to Tina.

Those were the last words Tina heard him say. Looking up at her from his strange position made Charles lose his balance. He tumbled to the ground. The train was upon them.

CHAPTER 2

The Mysterious Basket

The enormous train was between them. Tina could not see her brother. Her heart jumped to her throat as she looked through the spaces between the rushing freight cars. If only she could catch a glimpse of his breeches or even just his shoes. But the train was moving too fast. Tina quickly became dizzy and had to close her eyes for a few seconds.

Tina was older than Charles. She was supposed to be more mature and take more responsibility. Her parents expected her to look out for all her younger siblings, even the self-sufficient Charles. She should have grabbed Charles by the elbow and dragged him off the tracks when she first heard the train coming. But she was helpless now.

Finally the caboose rumbled past.

"Sixty-three," Charles announced triumphantly.

"Have you lost your mind, Charles?" Tina screamed as she ran across the tracks to where he stood.

"Sixty-three," he repeated. "That's longer than the last one."

Tina pushed out a hard breath to try to get her heart to slow down. She was relieved Charles was all right. But what had made him do such a dangerous thing in the first place? It was just like Charles to do whatever he wanted without thinking about what might happen next.

"Does it really matter whether a train has fifty-six or sixty-three cars?" Tina asked, with a mixture of relief and annoyance.

"Yes, it matters," Charles said in response to her question. Tina was not really expecting an answer. "The more cars it can pull, the stronger the engine is. Sometimes, of course, the train can't go very fast if it has too many cars for the engine or if the cars have a heavy load. Livestock, for instance, weighs a lot more than shoes. And, of course, anything made of steel is the heaviest of all. But I would think that even a train loaded down with heavy goods would be faster than your silly boats."

"Would you forget about the boats—and the train, too, for that matter?" Tina hissed. "You could have been killed."

"But I didn't get hurt, did I?" Charles retorted. "So what are you so worried about?"

"That was a foolish thing to do."

Charles looked at Tina and raised his eyebrows. "No one is safe all the time, Tina."

Tina rolled her eyes and sighed. "Charles, we've wandered too far from home. I'm hot and I'm tired. Mama will be looking for us to sit down and eat supper pretty soon."

Charles kicked at a railroad tie. It held solid. "I suppose you're right. But let's stop at the station on the way back into town."

"No!" Tina nearly shouted. "We're too far north. We're going home. Straight home."

This time she stepped behind Charles, grabbed his shoulders firmly with her hands, and pointed him toward downtown Cincinnati.

A bluish gray haze rose from the smokestacks that formed the skyline of Cincinnati. Puffs of fresh smoke rose, first from one factory, then another, then another. On hot days, the smoke seemed to rise a few feet and then settle. On a day with no breeze, the smoke and fumes from the manufacturing plants engulfed the city.

"I don't think people should have to work in the factories on Saturdays," Charles declared. "If I were in charge, I would give everyone the day off."

Tina smiled. "I thought you were in such a hurry to get those shoes to Chicago. If the factories closed on Saturday, the folks in Chicago would have to wait."

Charles made a face. "I don't care if I never see another pair of shoes." He stopped just long enough to lift his left foot and examine his shoe, made out of heavy leather with thick soles. They laced up tightly around his ankles. "Mama just bought these for me. I'm supposed to wear them all the time. But I don't see why I should have to wear shoes when it's not even cold outside. For all I care, they could shut down the shoe factories in the summer."

"Then there would be no shoes ready for the winter," Tina responded.

Charles rolled his head to one side. "Do you always have to be so sensible? Safe and sensible. That's Christina Fisk."

Tina did not respond. She did not want to begin an argument. She just wanted to get home.

"They could keep the pork houses open every day, though," Charles said, continuing their conversation but changing the subject. "I love roasted pork. I can't get enough of it."

"It's because of people like you that Cincinnati is called 'Porkopolis,' " Tina said.

"Cincinnati is called lots of things," Charles said. "But you have to admit, it's a great city. The Queen City of the West!" He glanced around. "We really are a long way from home."

They trudged a long way after that, moving east toward the center of the city. At one point, Charles sat down at the side of the road and pulled off his shoes. Tying the laces together, he slung them over one shoulder. Tina was tempted to do the same, but she knew her mother would disapprove of a thirteen-year-old girl walking around town barefoot. Sighing, she wiped the sweat off her face with one sleeve.

They were on the edge of the German section of town now. Tina had been there before with her cousin Meg.

Actually Meg was her mother's cousin. The daughter of Uncle Ben and Aunt Emma, Meg was grown up now—almost twenty-two years old. Aunt Emma's parents were German, so Meg knew a lot of the people in the German part of Cincinnati. When she'd been with Meg, Tina had gone up and down Vine Street, which ran straight through the center of the German section.

A young woman crossed the road in front of Tina and Charles, with four children huddling behind her. Over her shoulder, she softly gave out instructions in German.

"Do you think she speaks any English?" Charles asked.

"I doubt it, but why does it matter what she speaks?" Tina responded.

"I've heard some grown-ups say that people who come to America from Europe should learn to speak English and act like Americans."

"But most of the people in America came from somewhere else," Tina said, "just like a lot of people in Cincinnati came from somewhere else. I think that's part of what makes Cincinnati an interesting place to live."

"Do you know why people come here?" Charles asked.

Tina groaned. "I have a feeling you're going to say it has something to do with the railroad."

Charles grinned. "That's right. The railroad makes Cincinnati a good place to do business and a good place to make a living."

Tina shook her head. "You never give up, do you?"

They turned south and continued on. Tina calculated that they could be home in another half hour, if they did not dawdle.

"Did you see that?" Charles asked.

"See what?"

"The black man over there. He looks nervous."

Tina looked in the direction in which Charles nodded his head. A bearded black man, perhaps forty years old, stood on a corner, pressed against a building. His eyes roamed back and forth, as if searching for something.

"He's probably just waiting for someone," Tina guessed.

"Like a slave catcher, you mean."

"No! I meant a friend or a relative."

"How can you be sure?"

"It's not any of our business what that man is doing out here. He has a perfect right to be on a public street."

"Except if he's an escaped slave. He's pretty far away from the part of town where the black people live. That's way down by the river."

"Charles! If Papa and Mama heard you talk like that, they would be shocked."

"All I meant was that maybe he looks so nervous because he's not free."

"There could be a hundred things making him nervous—if he even is nervous."

"But what if he is a slave?"

"This is Cincinnati. We don't have slaves here."

"Christina Fisk, you know as well as I do that lots of runaway slaves come through Cincinnati. Uncle Tim talks about it all the time."

"Why would a runaway slave stand out in the middle of the street in broad daylight?" Tina asked.

"Oh, never mind." Charles turned away. "You're too

sensible for your own good."

"It wouldn't hurt you to show some responsibility once in awhile," Tina said sternly.

"Don't scold me! You're not my mother."

After that, they did not say much to each other. They made their way silently through the streets. The afternoon sun was waning, but the effort of walking so far kept Tina perspiring. At last they were getting closer to their own neighborhood. They passed a row of shops where their mother often sent them on errands.

"Hello, Mr. Stevens," Tina said cheerily. She perked up at the sight of the owner of the hat shop. She always enjoyed going in his store when her mother was picking out a new hat. Someday soon, she hoped, her mother would let her choose a hat for herself and exchange her girlish bonnet for something more sophisticated.

"Let's stop by Uncle Tim's office," Charles suggested. These were the first words he had spoken to her in nearly twenty minutes. "We can get a drink of water there."

"For once you have a good idea," Tina agreed.

They quickened their steps, turned the corner, and came to Tim Allerton's law office. Charles grasped the knob and leaned into the door with his shoulder. The door did not move.

"It's locked," Charles announced.

"What do you mean, it's locked?" Tina challenged. "Uncle Tim is always here on Saturdays."

"Well, he's not here today."

Unconvinced, Tina pressed her face against the glass of the front window. She saw no one, not Uncle Tim, not his assistant, not the young black woman who cleaned the office on the weekends.

"He's not here," Tina said.

Charles rolled his eyes.

"Okay, so you were right. I'm sorry." Tina's apology was curt. "I'm just so hot and thirsty." She turned to lead the way toward home.

As she turned the corner to the main street again, Tina wiped the sweat out of her eyes. For a split second, she could not see where she was going—just long enough to run into someone.

"Oh, I'm so sorry," she said profusely, opening her eyes wide now. "I didn't see you—Sarah! What are you doing here?"

"Thou art not the only one to do errands for thy mother," Sarah replied. At fifteen, Tina's Quaker friend was tall, reserved, and self-controlled. Wearing a simple dark cotton dress and a white bonnet, she carried a basket over one arm. As she spoke, she deftly covered the contents with a cotton cloth. Sarah and Tina had become friends several years ago when Sarah's mother had been ill and Tina's father had treated her.

"You don't live anywhere near here," Charles said. "Your farm is way on the east side of town, out Deer Creek Road. Aren't there any shops closer to your house?"

"My mother was quite specific in her instructions," Sarah said.

"What did you have to come all the way over here for?" Charles persisted in his questions. He reached out to lift the edge of the cloth Sarah had just placed over the basket.

Unflustered, Sarah stepped back ever so slightly so that Charles's fingertips missed the basket.

"Charles," Tina chided, "why are you bothering my friend?"

"I just wanted to know what was so important that she had to come all the way over here."

"It's not any of your business, so leave Sarah alone."

" 'Tis all right, Christina," Sarah said. "Thou hast no need to be sharp with thy brother." She stood with her free hand resting lightly on the top of the basket.

"That's right," Charles said emphatically. "Don't be sharp with thy brother."

Tina decided to change the subject. "We haven't had a good visit together in a long time, Sarah."

"This is quite true. Why dost thou not come to my house one day this week?"

"I could come on Wednesday," Tina said eagerly, "right after school."

"I shall look forward to thy visit." Sarah smiled softly. "Pray, excuse me, my mother will be waiting for me."

"Yes, and we must get home, too," Tina said. "I'll see you on Wednesday."

Serenely, Sarah glided down the street, keeping her basket level.

"What do you suppose is in that basket?" Charles asked.

"I said before that it's none of your business," Tina said.

"She has a secret," Charles said. "She didn't want me to see what was in that basket. She's not carrying vegetables."

CHAPTER 3

Danger for Uncle Tim

"Isn't that Uncle Tim's carriage?" Charles asked as they approached their home. He gestured down the block toward a polished carriage with soft leather seats, hitched to a young, coal black horse.

"Yes, and that's Uncle Ben's horse over there." Tina pointed to a gray mare contentedly munching on a small pile of hay placed in front of it.

Charles and Tina looked at each other, their eyes wide.

"Oh, no! I've done it again! I've forgotten something important," Charles moaned. "Were we supposed to be home for something? Is it someone's birthday? A family dinner?"

Tina furrowed her eyebrows and shook her head. "I

would have remembered something like that."

"And you would have reminded me about it a hundred times," Charles said, smiling slightly.

Tina did not return the smile. Something was wrong. Paying no attention to the heat that had bothered her all afternoon, she raced toward her house.

They reached the front steps together and jostled against one another to be the first one to the porch and through the door. Despite her smaller size and bulky skirt, Tina managed to get there first. She burst into the front room and immediately halted. Everyone was there—all the relatives. She glanced back over her shoulder at Charles, who had stumbled to a stop right behind her. He could now see for himself that the room was full.

"Is everybody a day early for Sunday dinner?" Charles whispered.

Uncle Tim and Aunt Dot sat together on a settee. Tina looked around for their children, three-year-old Daniel and two-year-old Elise. She did not see them. But she did not see her own twin brother and sister, either. The four of them were probably off somewhere else in the house together.

Across from Tim and Dot were Tina's mother's uncle, Ben Allerton, and his wife, Emma, with two of their children. Fred, twenty years old, and Julia, seventeen, sat stiffly in straightback chairs from the dining room. Their older sister, Meg, was missing.

Tina's father, Dr. Kevin Fisk, paced across the fireplace at the head of the room. Tina became even more alarmed. Papa never paced. He was a doctor; he faced crisis situations all the time. He did not get flustered. Something was definitely wrong. Tina's instinct told her to go find her mother to learn what was going on.

No one seemed to notice when Tina and Charles entered or when they began to move across the room. Tina slowly walked toward the kitchen, cocking her ear to listen to snatches of conversation along the way.

"You must take this seriously, Tim," Papa said sternly.

"You've had letters like this before, haven't you?" asked Uncle Ben. "Nothing ever came of them."

"This one has a more personal tone," Aunt Dot explained.

Tina could see that Uncle Tim was holding a piece of paper—no doubt the letter they were all talking about.

Tina turned to whisper something to Charles, but he was gone. She rotated her head around the room. He was nowhere around. How did he disappear so fast? Shrugging her shoulders, Tina continued her trek toward the kitchen.

When she pushed open the swinging door to the kitchen, Tina found her mother at the cutting counter with a knife in her hand.

"Oh, good, Tina, there you are," Mama said. "I could really use your help."

"Of course, Mama." Tina took the knife. "But what is going on?"

"I haven't really got time to explain just now. You'll have to be patient." Mama set a loaf of bread in front of Tina. "Can you slice this, please? And get a stack of the good plates out of the cupboard."

"Are we having company for dinner, Mama?" Tina whacked the end off the loaf of bread.

"No, not for dinner. I just thought a bit of refreshment

would ease everyone's mind."

Mama picked up a tray of fruit, and before Tina could speak again, her mother was gone.

"She's in quite a frenzy, isn't she?"

Tina turned to see her cousin Meg sitting on a stool in the corner. She had not noticed her before.

"Oh, hello, Meg." Tina stepped over to kiss her cousin's cheek. "I wondered where you were when I saw the rest of your family in the other room."

"I felt the need to retreat for a few minutes."

"So you came to the kitchen with my mother?" Tina laughed. "That's not much of a retreat."

"At least I can feel useful in here." Meg was slicing more fruit. "There is nothing I can do for Tim out there."

Tina reached up to open a cupboard and get down a stack of her mother's good dishes—the ones they only used on important occasions. She still did not know what was going on right now.

"Can you tell me—"

Tina's question was interrupted when Daria and David, her twin four-year-old brother and sister, burst into the room.

"Tina's home!" the twins squealed.

On seeing their sister, the little ones hurled themselves at her. Tina barely managed to set the good plates on the kitchen table before losing her balance. The twins' matching brown heads were soon buried in the folds of Tina's skirt.

"We asked Mama where you were," Daria said, pouting. "But she said we must be patient."

"We don't like to be patient," David said. "It takes too long."

Tina laughed. "Yes, being patient means you have to wait."

"Let's go for a walk!" Daria cried.

"I want to go outside," David declared.

Tina sighed and stooped down to talk to the twins, one arm around each of them.

"I've been out walking with Charles all afternoon," she explained, "and right now I think Mama needs me to stay here and help her for a little while. I've just promised her I would slice some bread."

Tina looked from one pair of wide brown eyes to the other. "How about if I give you the first slices? The bread is fresh, just the way you like it."

"Fresh bread, fresh bread, fresh bread," the twins chanted. Tina was always amazed that they could begin a unison appeal at precisely the same moment.

"Here, you sit at the table," Tina pulled out two chairs.

The twins clambered up and sat expectantly. Quickly, Tina cut off two slices of bread. She made sure they were thick enough to keep the twins busy for a few minutes and then slathered them with butter. Having quieted the twins by presenting them with their bread, she quietly turned back to Meg.

"You're very good with them," Meg said, smiling.

Tina shrugged. "Thank you. What's going on, Meg?" she asked. "Why is everyone here, and why is my mother in such a state?" She carried the bread and the cutting board to the end of the kitchen where Meg was working. She had a feeling that the twins did not need to hear all the details that she hoped Meg would reveal.

"Tim got a letter," Meg said quietly.

"Yes, but from whom? About what?"

"It's from someone who knows how opposed he is to slavery and how hard he is working to abolish it."

"That could be anyone in Cincinnati," Tina observed. "Uncle Tim has been very public with his opinions. What did the letter say?"

"It's a threat," Meg said, her voice so low that Tina could barely hear. She glanced at the twins. They had butter smeared on their faces, but they seemed content for the time being.

"What kind of threat?"

"He was told not to go to a certain meeting with other abolitionist lawyers," Meg explained, "or there would be consequences."

"Mama doesn't tell me everything," Tina said, "but I heard your father say that Uncle Tim has gotten other letters like this one."

Meg nodded. "Yes, but not exactly like this one. He's had two other letters that threatened his law practice. One threatened to burn down his building, but nothing came of it. But this letter said that harm would come to Daniel and Elise—by name. It's from someone who knows the family, not just Uncle Tim."

"Daniel and Elise? Someone would harm them? Where are they?"

"For now, Tim and Dot have hidden the children away with the Lankford cousins."

"The Lankfords?" Tina asked. "We hardly ever see them anymore."

"That's exactly why the children will be safe there. They are such distant cousins that not many people realize Tim is related to them." Meg began arranging her fruit pieces on a platter. "Of course Tim and Dot wanted everyone in the family to know, just in case there should be any danger to anyone else."

Tina's eyes widened. "Do you think there is?"

Meg shrugged one shoulder slightly. "The kinds of things that Uncle Tim is involved in can be very dangerous. He's my cousin. I grew up hearing about the dangerous situations he got himself into. He even got my brother Fred involved with the Underground Railroad once. I know some people in town are really angry with Tim."

"But that's no reason to threaten two innocent little children," Tina protested.

"It doesn't make sense to me, either." Meg looked over at Tina's bread. "Are you just about done? We should take these things out to the other room before your mother comes looking for them."

"Why does she think she has to feed everyone at a time like this?" Tina asked.

"She just wants people to be comfortable and cared for," Meg answered. She picked up her fruit tray. "Shall we go?"

"We go! We go!" the twins said.

"Go ahead, Meg," Tina said. "I'll have to clean their faces first."

A few minutes later, having given the twins a stern lecture about appropriate behavior, Tina joined the rest of the family in the other room. Graciously, she offered plates and passed the bread around. Then, satisfied she had done what her mother wanted her to do, she returned to her duty with the twins. Tina lifted both twins onto a cushion in the bay window behind the row of chairs where the rest of Meg's family sat. She sat with one arm around each of them and tried to listen to the conversation.

"Situations like this one will never end unless we do away with slavery once and for all," Uncle Tim said emphatically. "As long as slavery continues to exist in the South—and possibly in new territories—there will be violence over this issue."

"But you cannot abolish slavery all by yourself," Uncle Ben argued. "Perhaps there is a time to take some prudent caution for the sake of your family."

"And I have done so. I believe my children are out of the reach of harm. They will be safe until we get to the bottom of this."

"But what about you?" Uncle Ben pressed. "What will become of your children if something happens to you?" Uncle Ben's eyes caught Aunt Dot's and held them. "And what of your wife?"

"I am in full agreement with my husband's position," Aunt Dot said. "My family was involved in abolitionist activities long before I married Tim. I don't want to back down now."

Papa paused in his pacing and leaned against the mantle. "No one disputes Tim's political position," he said. "We're just concerned for the safety of your family."

"More bread!"

Tina clamped her hand over the mouth of the protesting twin. "Shhh," she whispered to her little sister. "We'll have more bread in a little while." She loosened her hold on Daria's mouth but did not move her hand away completely. If Tina had any concerns that the twins were hearing something that might frighten them, those fears were relieved. Obviously the two younger Fisks were still thinking about what awaited them in the kitchen. With a serious glance at both children, Tina turned her attention back to the adult conversation.

"And what of the safety of the runaway slaves?" Uncle Tim was asking. "Many of them have come north because they do not want to be separated from their families. They have a right to be treated as the human beings that they are."

"We all believe in what you are doing," Papa said. "But technically, helping runaway slaves is illegal. You cannot ignore the dangers that come with doing it."

On the other side of Tina, David began to unbutton his shirt. Tina knew what was coming next. She released her hold on Daria to stop David from removing his shirt and flinging it across the room.

"More bread!" Daria said again.

"Shhh!"

"More bread!" Daria whispered.

"Okay, okay, we'll get more bread," Tina whispered, quickly buttoning David's shirt. "But be quiet."

Tina wondered where Charles had gone off to. If he was not interested in the discussion, he could at least help out with Daria and David. But, as usual, Charles was never around when he was needed most.

Chapter 4
The Fighting Twins

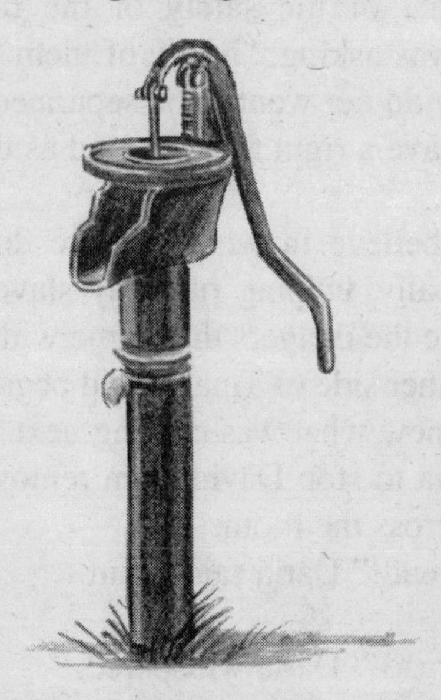

"So you're back," Meg said as Tina entered the kitchen again with the twins in tow.

"They didn't last very long out there," Tina said. "It was worse than taking them to church."

"More bread!" Daria said. "You promised we could have more bread."

"Yes, I did, and you may," Tina said. "Get back up in your chairs." She turned back to her cousin. "But why did you come back in here? Aren't you finished chopping fruit?"

Meg laughed. "Yes, I've done my duty with the fruit. I thought perhaps your mother could use a hand getting the kitchen straightened up and a meal started. I assume that you all plan to eat tonight."

It was Tina's turn to laugh. "These two may not need any supper if they keep this up." She set a slice of buttered bread in front of each twin. She found a pitcher of fresh milk among the clutter on the sideboard and filled twin mugs.

"At the rate things are going, you could be eating quite late," Meg said, "so perhaps it's just as well to fill their stomachs now. If you want to go back in the other room, I can keep an eye on them."

"Thanks, but that's okay. I heard enough to know what's going on. I'll just help you clean up in here."

"It's hard to know what to think, isn't it?" Meg said.

Tina took a rag and began scooping up bread crumbs from the butcher-block sideboard. "I know Uncle Tim believes in what he does. And I guess your parents and my parents do, too. But your father is right: what if something happens to Uncle Tim? What would become of his family?"

"It might seem as if Tim is being stubborn, or even foolish," Meg said as she wiped off the knife she had been using. "I used to think that. Now I think that what he does is brave."

Tina started sweeping the floor. "Sometimes it's hard to tell the difference between brave and foolish," she muttered. "Today Charles scared me half to death standing too close to a train passing by. He probably thought he was brave. But I think that he was being foolish."

Meg nodded. "Yes, because what did Charles accomplish by standing so close to a moving train?"

"Nothing!"

"That's exactly my point."

Tina stopped sweeping and leaned on the broom. "So if Uncle Tim is accomplishing something—for the slaves—then what he is doing is not foolish. It's brave. Is that what you are saying?"

"I think so."

"But where does safety fit in? He can be so busy looking after the safety of other people that he puts himself in danger."

"I suppose he thinks that the need to keep the other people safe is so great that it is worth the risk of danger to himself."

"Do you agree with that?"

Meg was wiping off the table and stopped midmotion. "I know I have the same beliefs that Tim has about slavery. I believe it's wrong. I don't think God meant for people to own other people and treat them like property."

"I have a friend at school who moved here from Kentucky," Tina said. She started sweeping again. "She thinks God created the white people to be better than the black people, so there's nothing wrong with slavery. She says using slaves helps the economy of the Southern states.

Without slaves, everyone would be poor. She doesn't think God wants her family to be poor."

Meg was nodding again. "Yes, I know people who say the same things."

"My friend knows all about God. She went to a big church in Kentucky. She's a really nice person. I like her a lot. But I don't understand what she thinks about slavery."

"It's very complicated."

"You never answered my question," Tina said. "Do you agree with Uncle Tim about taking risks?"

"I wish I could answer that. I guess I'm still trying to figure out where my limits would be."

"Mama always tells Charles to walk away from a fight," Tina said. "He gets it in his head that he can beat somebody up if another boy is bothering him at school, and she tells him that it's better just to walk away."

"Well, most of the time it is."

"But not always?"

Meg shook her head ever so slightly. "No. Not always."

The kitchen door swung open and Mama stuck her head in. "Oh, it looks wonderful in here. I wasn't expecting you to clean up. Thank you, both of you, for all your help this afternoon."

"I'm glad to help, Pamela," Meg said.

"Your folks are leaving now, Meg," Mama said. "They're out on the porch."

"I'm coming right this minute," Meg said. She reached behind her waist to untie the apron she had been wearing and put it on a hook in the corner.

Tina swiped at the faces of Daria and David, once

again covered with butter.

"Come say good-bye to everyone," Tina said.

"Good-bye to everyone!" Daria said.

Tina sighed. "You know what I mean. Show everyone your good manners."

David hopped down from his chair. "I have very good manners," he said, and he marched out of the kitchen toward the departing relatives.

Tina followed with Daria and Meg. By the time she reached the front porch, David was going down the line shaking hands with his cousins and aunts and uncles. Tina couldn't help smiling at his effort.

Daria squirmed out of Tina's arms. "I can do that, too!" And she started with Aunt Emma and made her way through the line of relatives as well. When she reached her Aunt Dot and cousin, Julia, she bestowed hugs as well as handshakes.

Smiling as she watched Daria, Tina did not see Meg come to stand beside her. Meg squeezed Tina's shoulder gently.

"Let's go for a carriage ride soon," Meg said, "just the two of us."

"I'd like that," Tina said smiling. Her heart raced slightly at the thought that her grown-up cousin Meg was treating her like an adult.

When the last of the relatives had said good-bye and the Fisk family stood on the porch alone, Papa rubbed his hands together. "I'm sure we have some things we should be doing around here," he said.

"Perhaps we should have invited everyone to stay for

supper," Mama said as she watched her brother's carriage disappear around the corner. "It's an awkward time of day to send everyone home, and with such heavy thoughts on their minds. A good meal would have helped."

Papa put an arm around his wife's shoulder. "One of the things I love most about you is the way you love to take care of everyone."

Tina smiled at the tender moment between her parents.

"Let's get this household in order again," Papa said. "What needs to be done?"

"I haven't seen Charles," Mama said. "Didn't he come home with you, Tina?"

Tina nodded. "He came home with me, but then he disappeared again right away."

"The railroad station," her parents said in unison.

"Probably," Tina agreed. "We walked the tracks this afternoon, and he wanted to go by the station. I didn't want to do it."

"I want to go to the railroad station!" David said.

"Me, too," Daria chimed in. "Let's go to the railroad station."

Papa grabbed his two youngest children and whirled them around one time. "We can't go today. It's getting late. But maybe one day next week."

The twins squealed their agreement.

"I don't suppose his chores were done before Charles disappeared," Papa said doubtfully as he set the twins down.

Tina and her mother burst into laughter. "When was the last time Charles did his chores on a Saturday?" Tina asked.

"Or any day," Mama added. "We must do something to teach that boy some responsibility."

"I'll help you with supper, Mama," Tina offered.

"We'll do something easy tonight," Mama said. "Perhaps we'll just work on the bread left over from this afternoon. I have some drippings I could use to make gravy."

Tina giggled. "If you're looking for your leftover bread, you can look at those two right there." She pointed at the grinning twins. "They stuffed themselves. In fact, I can't imagine that they could eat anything more."

"More bread!"

"More bread!"

Tina growled playfully. "How could you possibly eat any more bread?"

Papa tickled Daria one last time. "I'll go find Charles."

"Come on, twins," Mama coaxed. "Let's go clean up properly." She herded them into the house.

Tina was glad for a few minutes to herself, and she knew exactly what she wanted to do. She scampered down the porch steps and around the side of the house. With a burst of glee, she grasped the red handle of the old water pump. Even though the Fisks had water piped into the kitchen now, Tina loved the old pump. She pumped the red handle vigorously a few times, and soon the water began to flow.

The first thing she did was splash some on her face. As cold as it was, she did not flinch. All afternoon, on the long walk home, she had pined for a cold drink. Then when she got home, in the midst of the chaos, she forgot to get it. Now she cupped her hands under the pump and swallowed gulps of cool refreshment. Alone with her thoughts, she realized how tired she was. She let herself fall back into the grass and gave way to her weariness.

The kind of thing that Tim is involved in can be very dangerous. Meg's words rang in Tina's ears. Tina had grown up hearing her Uncle Tim talk about the abolitionist cause. She could say "abolitionist" almost before she could say "Christina Fisk." She had always been proud of her uncle. He was a successful attorney in Cincinnati. He probably could have gone anywhere in the country and given his family a good life. Tina was glad that he chose to stay in Cincinnati.

But now, would it be safe for him to stay here? If he continued to meet with other abolitionist lawyers, would Daniel and Elise ever be able to come home? And was it fair to make two small children go stay with strangers—even if the Lankfords were distant cousins—so that Uncle Tim could carry out his work?

As tired as she was, Tina's mind churned with questions. She agreed with her parents that Charles needed to learn some responsibility. But perhaps her uncle had taken on too much responsibility.

Reluctantly, Tina pulled herself to her feet. By now her mother would be wondering if she, too, had gone astray.

As soon as she stepped inside the back door, Tina groaned. The twins were at it again. She heard their high-pitched voices from the dining room.

"I want to play with it!"

"No, it's mine, and I want it."

"But I found it. You didn't have it."

"But it's mine. I don't want you to have it."

Just as she was about to go into the dining room to see what she could do to prevent a major battle, she heard her mother's soothing tones. Gradually the four-year-olds settled down. Mama continued talking. Her voice was too muffled for Tina to hear the words, but Tina knew her mother was talking about sharing and generosity. That's what she had always talked about when Tina and Charles were small. In another moment, the twins were playing happily again.

Tina shook her head and wished that all fighting could be solved so easily. The dispute between Uncle Tim and his enemies, the friction between the North and the South—what would it all come to?

Chapter 5
Attacked!

Tuesday came. So far nothing had happened to Uncle Tim. His children were still with the Lankfords. Tina hated to think of Daniel and Elise being away from their parents, but she knew the Lankfords would take good care of them.

That day after school, Charles rushed up to Tina. "Let's take a little side trip on our way home," he said.

"No, Charles. We are not going to stop by the railroad station." Tina sighed with impatience.

"Come on, Tina," Charles protested. "For once I wasn't thinking of the railroad. I was thinking we could stop by the Lankfords' house and see how Daniel and Elise are doing. Please?"

"Hush!" Tina hissed, glancing around quickly to see who might have heard Charles's words. "Do you want the whole world to know where they're hidden?"

"Oops!" Charles put his hand to his mouth and looked around in alarm. "I didn't think."

"No, you didn't," his sister agreed. "But I think your idea's a good one. Let's go."

Tina and Charles had walked just a couple blocks when she got the uncomfortable feeling that they were being followed. She glanced back and saw a man leaning against a building. Odd. He hadn't been there when they'd walked by seconds before.

"Charles," Tina whispered. "Don't look now, but I think we're being followed. Let's stop by the confectionary and pretend to look in the window at the candy. If the man I saw leaning against that building we just passed is still behind us, we'll have to figure out a way to get away from him."

Charles rolled his eyes. "Don't you think you're overreacting just a bit, Tina? I mean, who would bother following a couple school kids to find Uncle Tim's children?"

"Maybe I am being overly cautious," Tina admitted. "But under the circumstances, I'd rather be extra careful than assume there are no dangers and put Daniel and Elise at risk."

"I suppose," Charles said grudgingly.

Just then Charles and Tina reached the confectionary. Tina stood to Charles's left so she would have a clear view of the area they'd just passed. As they stood by the window, she glanced up the street. A chill ran down her spine. Leaning against a building a block away was the same man she'd seen before.

"He's still with us," Tina reported to Charles. "And I can't imagine why anyone would go from block to block, leaning against all the buildings, can you?"

Charles looked at his sister, then shook his head. "You may be right. Let's head up to the mercantile, slip out the back door, and run down toward the landing. If he doesn't lose sight of us in the store, it'll be harder for him to follow us near the landing, where it's so much busier."

"Good idea," Tina agreed. "Let's go."

Quickening their pace, Tina and Charles turned at the next corner and reached the mercantile in record time. As they entered the door, Tina glanced back over her shoulder. The man was half a block behind them.

"Come on," she urged her brother. They hurried through the mercantile and managed to get out the back door before the mysterious man had reached the front entrance. Quickly, they went to the back corner of the building and peered around to make sure he wasn't in sight.

"Follow me," Charles whispered. "I know these back alleys better than you."

Tina couldn't argue the point. She gathered up her long skirts and followed her younger brother as he raced through the alleys halfway to the landing. Then he turned out onto a main street. They paused to catch their breath and look for the man who had been following them. He was nowhere to be seen.

"Good," Charles said. "Now we can get on to the Lankfords."

They turned back up toward the residential area where the Lankfords lived, checking occasionally to make sure they weren't being followed. At last they reached the front door of the Lankford home. Mrs. Lankford answered their knock.

"Tina! Charles!" she said. "What a surprise. And I can guess what I owe the honor of this visit to. Please come in."

As Tina and Charles entered the elegant home, Mrs. Lankford gave them a puzzled look. "Have you two run into trouble?" she asked. "You're both so flushed, and Tina, I don't think I've seen your hair this disheveled since you were younger than Elise."

Just then, Daniel and Elise burst into the hallway. "Charles! Tina!" they screamed.

"Charles," Tina suggested, "why don't you take the children to the playroom, and I'll tell Mrs. Lankford about our little bit of excitement."

Charles opened his mouth as if to protest, but then stopped. He looked at the young children with understanding and smiled at his older sister. "Some things they don't need to know about, right?"

"Right."

"Okay, Daniel, Elise," Charles shouted, making Tina and Mrs. Lankford wince. "Let's play trains in the playroom. Last one there's a rotten egg."

Mrs. Lankford shook her head as all three children went racing off. "I usually don't permit running in the house," she confided to Tina, "but under the circumstances I think it's just as well for them to get rid of a little steam. Now come with me to the kitchen. We can have some tea and you can tell me what happened."

When Tina had finished her story, Mrs. Lankford shook her head. "You both handled the situation wisely," she said, "and I'm glad you noticed the man before you got anywhere near this neighborhood. But. . ." Her voice trailed off.

"You think it would be better for us not to visit again while the children are here?" Tina said.

"I'm afraid so," Mrs. Lankford said. "Much as the children enjoy spending time with you and Charles, I'm afraid we have to put their safety first."

"Of course," Tina said. "But I'm not sure how happy Charles will be about this."

Charles wasn't happy about the decision, but it was soon clear that he wouldn't have any choice in the matter. Once Mama and Papa heard about Charles's and Tina's adventure, they were firm in their decision.

"Neither of you are to go within five blocks of the Lankford home," Papa said sternly, looking at both children. "As Mrs. Lankford said, you handled today's events well, but we don't want you to be in such a situation again. We don't know who these people are. We only know that they're willing to threaten two little children because of your uncle Tim's beliefs. Who knows what they would do to you if they had caught you? So, no trips anywhere near the Lankfords. Do I make myself clear?"

"Yes, Papa," Tina said.

"Charles?"

"Yes, Papa," Charles said, a definite pout forming on his lips.

Life at the Fisk household quickly settled back to a normal routine that evening, although Tina's parents were very nervous. The twins were even more feisty and louder than usual, if that was possible. Or perhaps it just seemed that way to Tina because her mind was working so hard at sorting out confusing ideas. After the discussion about their trip to visit Daniel and Elise, Charles had been chastised about his long absences and frequent visits to the train station—and, of course, his homework, which he regularly forgot to do.

By Wednesday, Tina was ready for her afternoon with Sarah. For most of the afternoon, she looked out the small windows of the squarish, brick schoolhouse every few minutes, waiting for the words "class dismissed." She heard very little of the lecture on European history. She would have to ask a classmate about it later or do some extra reading to make up for her daydreaming. As soon as the teacher released the students, Tina scrambled to collect her things and dashed out the door.

Tina enjoyed the walk to Sarah's house. The Henrys lived on a farm at the very eastern edge of Cincinnati. Tina always felt like she was getting away from the city when she went to Sarah's house. But it was a bit far, which was one of the reasons that they did not see each other often.

Even at a hurried pace, it took Tina more than an hour to get there. Already she hoped that someone in Sarah's family would offer to take her home by wagon or carriage.

Tina turned down the dirt lane that led to Sarah's house. The white clapboards rose from the cornfield, a welcome sight to the arriving visitor. A wide, comfortable porch stretched across the front of the house and around one side. At almost any time of the day, some part of the porch was in the shade, and anyone needing relief from the heat of the sun could find it there. At both ends of the front porch, freshly painted stairs were like open hands reaching out to Tina, offering to enfold her in their security.

When she reached the porch, Sarah was there with a glass of lemonade.

"Thank you!" Tina said enthusiastically. She gulped the liquid and savored its coolness as it slid down her throat. She hardly noticed that there was not enough sugar in it.

"Thou hast walked a long way," Sarah said in her gentle voice. "I am glad to offer thee refreshment."

"I don't care how far it is," Tina said. "I'm always glad to come and see you." She smiled at her friend.

"I would be happy to come to thy house," Sarah said. "Perhaps the next time I have errands in town, we can meet."

Tina could not quite imagine Sarah at her house, fighting off the twins and putting up with Charles's nosy questions. No, it was better for Tina to come to Sarah. They could have a real conversation without interruptions or worrying about lamps getting knocked over.

Their families were very different. The Fisks went to a big church in Cincinnati, where the pastor prayed and preached and the congregation sang from a hymnal at specific times in the service. Sarah's family went to a simple meeting house, where they sat in silence with several other families until someone felt moved by the Spirit to say something. The Fisk household was noisy, with four children in the house and something always going on. Sarah was an only child, and her house was always peaceful. Or so it seemed to Tina. Sarah insisted it was not always that way.

In spite of the differences in their upbringing, Tina felt like she could be herself with Sarah, say anything she wanted to say, do anything she wanted to do. But it would not be that way if Sarah came to her house.

Sarah led the way to the front door and then showed Tina into a sitting room.

"I beg thee to be patient a few more minutes," Sarah said. "The chickens must be fed. Then I will be able to join thee until suppertime."

"Take thy time," Tina said. The words had slipped out in the Quaker fashion before Tina realized it. Sarah gave Tina an odd look.

Tina laughed nervously. "I'm sorry, Sarah. I did not mean to make fun of the way you speak. I find myself following your ways when I am here."

Sarah smiled graciously. "I take no offense from thy words. I know thy heart means well. Wilt thou wait for me here?"

Tina nodded. "I promise not to leave the room."

"I shall need only ten minutes or so."

So Tina was left on her own in a charming sitting room

in a Quaker home. She had been in this room only once before and remembered that she had found it intriguing. She welcomed the opportunity to examine the furnishings closely. The walls were paneled on the bottom half in dark wood polished to a lustrous shine. Tina dared graze it only with the lightest touch, lest she leave a fingerprint. The paneling was topped off by a wood border of intricate design, carved patiently and tediously over a period of several years.

Simple wooden chairs were arranged around the room. Sarah's father was a carpenter, as well as a farmer. He had a shop in town. Tina knew that Ezekiel Henry had made much of the furniture in the family's home. Admiring the curve of the backs of the chairs and the smoothly gliding rocker, Tina made a mental note to tell her Uncle Ben about Sarah's father. Perhaps the two carpenters already knew each other. If not, they surely ought to meet. Uncle Ben would have great appreciation for the craftsmanship of the furniture in this room.

One whole wall was lined with shelves and various cabinets, arranged in a pleasing display. Tina guessed that Mr. Henry had made most of these shelves as well. Many of them held books, more books than Tina had ever seen in one place. Sarah's mother, Rebecca Henry, was a great reader and lover of literature. Sarah often quoted what her mother had to say on various topics. With her head tilted to one side, Tina went from shelf to shelf, reading the spines of the books. She let the fingers of one hand trail behind her, lightly brushing against the edge of the shelves.

At the far end of the room, tucked into a corner, stood

a simple cabinet with no ornate carving and nothing to distinguish it. Yet somehow Tina was drawn to it, perhaps because of its simplicity. It was made of oak, Tina's favorite wood, with two doors on the top and two doors on the bottom. Rather than elaborate handles, the doors were opened by simple knobs that perfectly matched the wood of the cabinet.

"This is lovely," Tina said under her breath. Her fingers traced the edge of the cabinet. On impulse, and expecting to find more books, she pulled open one bottom door. To her surprise, the cabinet was empty, except for a ceramic vase with a chip at the top. She supposed that with so much other storage space in the room, this cabinet really was not needed. Yet it was beautiful, at least to Tina.

Suddenly Tina had a strange idea. She had promised Sarah that she would not leave the room. But perhaps she could have a little fun without breaking her promise. For once, Tina was grateful for her small size. If she were as big as most thirteen-year-olds, she would not be able to do what she planned to do just then. She pulled open the other bottom door and confirmed that her idea would work.

If she pulled her knees up under her chin and bent her head sideways, she could fit in the space of that empty cabinet.

Tina carefully slid the vase to a back corner and folded herself into the cabinet. With her fingers gripping the inside edges of the doors, she pulled them shut behind her.

After a moment, Tina's eyes began to adjust to the dark. A thin stream of light filtered through the space where the two doors came together on the outside of the cabinet. Tina discovered that if she looked straight out through the crack, she could see the doorway of the room. She would be able to see Sarah's entrance and the expression on her face when she found Tina gone.

Tina snickered under her breath. Playing hide and seek at her age! What would her mother think? Tina did not care. She thought it was fun, and the empty cabinet was irresistible.

When she thought she heard footsteps coming, she held her breath and squinted through the crack. But the steps passed by in the hall. *That must have been Mrs. Henry,* Tina thought. She had not counted on anyone but Sarah discovering her. She hoped Mrs. Henry did not come into the room before Sarah returned. With her arms wrapped around her legs and her knees tucked under her chin, Tina could do little else but sit very still and wait.

Tina was sure that far more than ten minutes had passed by now. Sarah should have been back. What if Sarah had glanced in the room, discovered Tina missing, and went to look for her somewhere else in the house? Tina realized she could be scrunched up in the cabinet for a long time waiting for Sarah. Already her knees were starting to hurt.

But what if Sarah was simply taking a little longer with the chickens? She could come back at any second. Tina kept waiting.

Once again she heard footsteps. This time, though, she was sure they were going down the hall toward the kitchen. Mrs. Henry was passing by again, on her way back, Tina decided. *Come on, Sarah,* Tina thought. *This won't be any fun if you don't come back soon.*

For the third time, Tina heard footsteps. It was a lighter and smoother sound—much more like the way that Sarah walked. Tina grinned in the darkness and started to hold her breath.

Instead she screamed—or tried to. A hand over her mouth trapped the sound in Tina's throat. Her hands flew up from her knees to claw at the fingers that threatened her. No longer concerned about keeping quiet to surprise Sarah, Tina thrashed against the inside of the cabinet as much as the small space would allow her.

She stretched out one leg and was surprised at how far she was able to unfold it. Doing this allowed her to twist around and wrestle her opponent straight on. As she ripped the hand away from her face, Tina stared into two wide brown eyes with bright white circles around them. She tried to scream again.

Chapter 6
Sarah's Secret

Free from her opponent's grip, Tina threw herself against the inside of the door of the cabinet. There was no latch on the inside! And why should there be? No one ever opened a cabinet door from the inside—unless someone was foolish enough to do what Tina had done.

The door was stuck and would not budge. She pressed against it again, grunting as she did so. Still, it would not open. Tina looked over her shoulder. The pair of eyes was gone. Utter darkness surrounded her, save for the thin line of light creeping between the doors. Tina felt sure she was alone again. But she wanted out of the cabinet!

Tina peered anxiously through the crack in the doors. She knew she had heard footsteps just a moment ago. Why hadn't anyone come into the room? Sarah had been gone almost half an hour. Where was she?

"Sarah! Are you out there?" Tina pounded against the door with the palm of her hand. She did not care who discovered her foolishness. She just wanted out.

At last the door gave way. Tina tumbled out of the cabinet and landed in a heap on the floor. At first she was too stunned to move, but only for a second. What if whoever or whatever was in that cabinet tried to follow her out? She scrambled to her feet and slammed the door shut, then leaned against it with her slight body.

She stood like that for a few moments, breathing heavily, her eyes darting around the room. Where was Sarah?

Tina forced herself to take deep breaths. When she was little, her father used to tell her to do that when she was frightened. Gradually Tina's breathing and heart rate returned to normal. She heard no footsteps in the hall and no sounds from within the cabinet. Tina crossed the room and stood in the doorway. She looked in both directions down the hall. No one was in sight. She could not even hear anyone working in another room. It was as if she were alone in the house.

"Sarah?" she called, but not too loudly. She was still confused by what had happened. She thought about finding her way out back to the chicken coop to find Sarah and tell her what had happened.

But what had happened? Tina had no explanation. The cabinet was barely large enough for her to squeeze into. How could something else be in there—someone else? For it had been a human hand that covered her mouth and human eyes that she had stared into. How could she explain that to Sarah?

With new determination, Tina went back into the sitting room and strode over to the cabinet. Boldly she opened the doors and peered in. The chipped vase was in the corner where she had left it. The space looked like an ordinary empty cabinet. No one could possibly be in there.

But someone was in there.

Reaching into the cabinet, Tina pressed her fingertips against its walls, first along the top edge, then along the bottom edge. She rapped with her knuckles, then paused, as if she expected someone to return her knock. No one did—because no one was in there, she told herself. How could anyone be in there?

"But I am not imagining things," Tina said aloud. Frustrated, she slammed the cabinet doors shut and leaned her forehead against them.

"Christina?"

Tina whirled around to see Sarah standing behind her. After waiting so long to hear footsteps while she huddled in the cabinet, Tina had not heard Sarah coming.

"Christina, what's wrong?"

"Sarah, there is something—someone—in this cabinet."

"I assure thee, nothing is in that cabinet except an old vase that my mother cannot bear to part with."

Tina folded her hands in front of her waist and looked

her friend squarely in the face.

"Sarah, do you think I'm a sensible person?"

"Thou art one of the most sensible people I have ever met."

"Do you think I'm a liar?"

"Of course not. Thou tellest the truth, I am sure of it."

"Then why won't you believe me when I say there is something in the cabinet?"

Sarah squeezed her eyebrows together. "Hast thou looked in the cabinet?"

Tina moved her hands behind her waist. "Well, yes, I did look. And I saw the old vase. Then. . ."

"Yes?"

"Then I got in the cabinet."

"Thou wast in the cabinet?"

"I know it sounds silly now, but I was just going to play a trick on you."

"Thou wast in the cabinet?" Sarah repeated.

"Sarah, someone is in there!"

Sarah took a few steps toward the windows at the other end of the room. "The afternoon is beautiful," Sarah said. "We can get some more lemonade and go outside and enjoy it."

"Sarah, did you hear what I said?" Tina did not move away from the cabinet.

"My father has put a bench under the elm tree. It is a lovely place to sit and talk."

"I'm sure the bench is lovely," Tina said, "but I want to understand what is going on here. Why can't I see anyone when I open the door to the cabinet?"

"Perhaps because no one is in there."

Tina turned around and yanked open the door again. The vase was there—but it was back in the center of the space.

"Sarah, look, the vase!"

"Yes, I told thee it was there."

"But I moved it to the corner when I crawled in. Now it's back in the middle."

"Perhaps when thou climbed out—"

"No, I'm sure it was in the corner."

The gentle probing Tina had done earlier had not answered her questions. This time, she started banging on the inside walls of the cabinet.

Sarah quickly moved in and tried to grab Tina's arms. "Christina! What art thou doing? My father made this cabinet, and it is my mother's favorite."

Tina banged some more.

"You must stop!" Sarah demanded.

"Why, Sarah?" Tina asked, her voice rising. "Why must I stop? What do you know that you are not telling me?"

"It's just. . .just. . .the cabinet. I'm afraid thou wilt damage the cabinet."

"The cabinet is made out of oak. I can't hurt it with my hands."

"Please, Christina." Sarah glanced anxiously over her shoulder at the door.

"Okay, I'll stop," Tina said, and she did. "But I want you to explain to me what is going on. There was barely room for me in there, but someone else was in there, too. And someone did move that vase!"

"Tina, you are a sensible person. Think sensibly now."

"The other day when Charles and I saw you in the market, he thought you were hiding something in your basket. I thought his imagination was working too hard. But I'm starting to believe him."

"Please, Christina, please." Sarah was starting to sound desperate for Tina to move away from the cabinet—which only made Tina more curious.

"Hast thou a problem?" Mrs. Henry stood in the doorway, her hands pressed together in front of her and one eyebrow raised. Her long, dark dress fit tightly around the waist and flared out to the floor. Even on such a warm day, she wore long sleeves.

"Mother," Sarah said, stumbling over her words, "Christina is interested in the oak cabinet. I've explained that it is your favorite, that we should leave it alone."

"Thou hast spoken rightly," Mrs. Henry said. "I know that thou wilt be careful with the cabinet."

Tina tried to compose herself and decide what to say. If Sarah did not believe her, would Mrs. Henry believe her?

"It's a beautiful cabinet, Mrs. Henry," Tina said carefully and politely. "I understand that Mr. Henry built it. It's quite lovely."

"Yes, I have always thought so."

"My mother's uncle is a carpenter. I'm sure he would enjoy meeting your husband."

"Perhaps they shall meet some day."

"May I ask a few questions about the cabinet?" Tina glanced at Sarah, who was starting to squirm. Perhaps it would be better to forget what happened and go sit under the elm tree with her friend. But no, Tina decided, she had to know what really had happened.

Mrs. Henry gestured toward the wooden chairs. "Please, sit, and we shall talk."

Tina and Sarah sat side by side across from Mrs. Henry. Tina looked at Sarah, but Sarah did not want to meet Tina's gaze. Instead, Sarah stared at nothing in particular.

"What is thy question?" Mrs. Henry asked.

Tina swallowed hard and moistened her lips. "First, I must make a confession. While I was admiring this lovely room and the fine collection of books you have, I took far too much liberty with your belongings. I should never have touched the oak cabinet. Please forgive me."

"Thou art forgiven," Mrs. Henry said. "I'm sure no harm has been done."

Sarah turned toward Tina. "Perhaps now would be a good time for some refreshment." She jumped up from her chair and motioned that Tina should follow her.

"Thank you, Sarah, but not just yet."

Sarah sat down again, clearly uncomfortable.

Tina continued. "I am sorry for the liberties I took," she said sincerely, "but I crawled inside the cabinet to play a trick on Sarah."

"Thou wast inside the cabinet?" Mrs. Henry had the same tone of quiet alarm that Sarah's voice had held a few minutes earlier.

"Yes—and someone else is in there! Someone grabbed me."

"Mother," Sarah said, "of course I have explained that

there is nothing in the cabinet but thine old vase."

Mrs. Henry was silent for a moment, looking from Sarah to Tina and back to Sarah. Tina's heart starting pumping faster when she realized Mrs. Henry was not going to try to talk her out of believing what she said had happened. The silence stretched from seconds into minutes.

At last Mrs. Henry spoke. "Please tell me what happened. Everything."

With relief, Tina gave every detail—huddling in the dark, the hand over her mouth, the eyes staring back at her, the strange sensation of being able to stretch out her legs in that small space.

When Tina finished talking, Mrs. Henry said nothing. For a moment, she pressed her lips together and studied her hands in her lap. Then she slowly rose from her chair. Wordlessly, she crossed the room and shut the door to the hall. Then she went to the wall with windows looking out over the front yard. One by one, she pulled curtains down to cover the windows.

"Mother," Sarah said. "Are—"

Mrs. Henry cut her off. "It is time for Christina to know the truth."

Tina's heart raced even faster. The truth about what?

Mrs. Henry dropped the last curtain over the final window. The heavy curtains, once closed, had cut off the daylight. The room was swallowed up in a gray shadow.

"Light the lamp, please, Sarah," Mrs. Henry instructed.

Obediently, Sarah struck a match and lit a lamp on the table next to her.

Without speaking further, Mrs. Henry crossed to the

cabinet, opened the bottom doors, and put her hand inside.

Tina held her breath as she watched to see what would happen next. Gently, Mrs. Henry tapped on the back wall. Tap. Pause. Tap, tap. Pause. Tap. She waited a few seconds and repeated her action. Tap. Pause. Tap, tap. Pause. Tap. Then she stepped back away from the cabinet.

In the grayness of the room, Tina could barely make out what she saw. A small form, hardly bigger than her own, carefully climbed out of the cabinet and stood beside Mrs. Henry.

Tina leaped to her feet. She had been right all along!

Tina recognized the eyes, the wide brown eyes in circles of white. But this time she realized how frightened those eyes looked. They belonged to a thin young woman, probably not yet twenty years old—a black woman.

The truth began to sink in.

"Christina," Mrs. Henry said, "this is Tillie. She is from Georgia."

CHAPTER 7
Tillie's Story

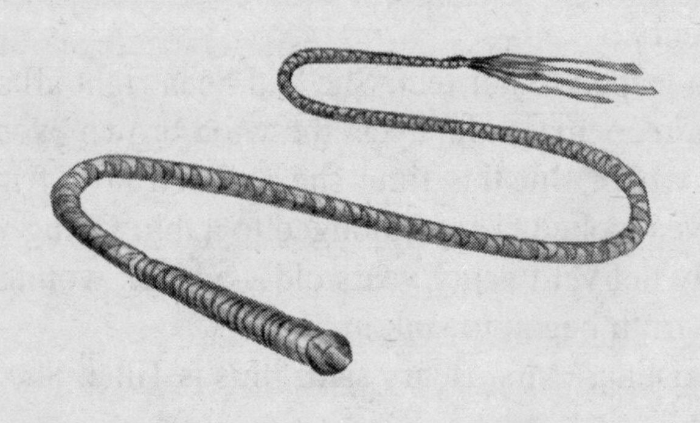

Tina did not know what to say.

"Tillie—I. . .I. . ."

"I am sorry about what I did to you," Tillie said softly. She did not look at Tina. She fixed her eyes on a spot on the floor in front of her. "I was scared. I didn't know what you were going to do."

"I. . .I understand," Tina said. "I was scared, too."

Mrs. Henry gestured toward the chairs. "Why don't we all sit down?"

Tina sat across from Tillie, fascinated. She had seen black people before, of course. Cincinnati had one of the largest black populations of any of the Northern cities. But a runaway slave! As far as she knew, she had never met a runaway slave before.

"Christina, our home is a stop along the Underground Railroad," Mrs. Henry said. "Tillie is going to be a passenger on the next train to Canada."

"I've heard my uncle talk about the Underground Railroad," Tina said in a small voice. "But I never. . .met anyone. . .before."

"I am well acquainted with thine uncle, Timothy Allerton," Mrs. Henry said. "He has referred passengers to us on several occasions."

Tina's eyes grew wide. "He has? I thought he was just working on changing the laws."

"Thine uncle is very involved in the abolitionist movement. He is one of our greatest friends." Mrs. Henry turned to Tillie. "This is why I thought it would be safe for thee to meet Christina. Be assured I will not endanger thy safety."

Tillie simply nodded. She was very frightened, Tina realized, and not sure what might happen next.

"I won't hurt you, either," Tina blurted out. "I never meant to cause any trouble for you. I'm sorry. I should have listened to Sarah and gone to sit under the elm tree."

"What's done is done," Mrs. Henry said. "Perhaps you would like to hear Tillie's story."

Yes! Tina thought. More than anything at that moment, she wanted to hear Tillie's story. But she restrained herself. "Only if Tillie wants to tell me," Tina said.

Tillie was still looking at the floor most of the time.

"Tillie?" Mrs. Henry asked softly, taking the young woman's hand.

Tillie nodded. "I'll tell you." And she began.

"I was born on a plantation in Georgia. I lived all my life there. My mama and daddy are still there, as far as I know. When I was a youngun, the master and missus brought me into the master's house to play with the little girl. Miss Samantha and I, we were friends, the best friends. The missus taught me to read right along with Miss Samantha. And she made me talk properly, not the way my mama and daddy had taught me. If I was going to be Miss Samantha's companion, I had to be suitable.

"When we got older, Miss Samantha got sent off to boarding school for weeks at a time. I was put to work, real work, for the first time. They trained me as a cook and a maid so I could help with whatever household work needed to be done. I knew I was lucky. I still went and slept with my mama and daddy every night, so I saw how the other slaves lived. I knew I was blessed to be a house worker and not a field hand. I ate my meals at the big house, and I got to touch nice things. They weren't my own things, of course, but they were nice. When Miss Samantha came home from school, she always brought me something. I was mighty blessed to work in the house and not out in the hard weather.

"When I was about ten, a new slave came to the plantation. Hubert was only about twelve—he was never sure when he was born—but he was big for his age, and strong. The master had bought him for a good price at the slave market in New Orleans and brought him home to work in the cotton fields."

Tillie paused and smiled ever so slightly.

"I knew Hubert was for me the minute I laid eyes on him.

When I was sixteen, we finally got married. It wasn't a real church wedding, of course. We couldn't do that, but we had the blessing of my parents and we had our own little ceremony with the black folks. And we were happy living together. All day long while I worked in the house, I looked forward to the nights when I could go be with Hubert and rub his aching muscles and cook him a good meal.

"Last year, we found out we were going to have a baby! We didn't tell anyone. The master would think the baby was his to do with as he wanted. I was real careful about what I ate and what I wore so I wouldn't start showing too soon. We knew that eventually the master would find out about the baby, but we wanted the secret to ourselves for a while.

"Then, one day while I was washing dishes in the kitchen, I overheard the master and the missus talking. He told her that he had found someone who had given him a good price for Hubert. The new master would come the next day to take Hubert away. He was going to go work on a farm in Alabama.

"I finished washing the dishes and straightened up the kitchen. I knew Hubert would still be out in the field. That was the longest day of my life—waiting until it was time to go home to our little lean-to and tell Hubert the news.

"Right away, we decided he had to leave—not to go to Alabama, but to be free. We had been lucky enough to be together for eight years on that plantation." Tillie started to cry. Mrs. Henry handed her a handkerchief. "I knew that the master would not change his mind. Nothing I could say would convince him not to sell Hubert. He had already taken the money from the new owner. That's when I knew I was a slave. I thought the master was happy for me when I married Hubert. But he didn't care about my feelings. He was sending my very heart away from me just for money. He could sell me off at any moment, too.

"If Hubert and I had to be separated, it was better that he run for his freedom than go to Alabama. I tried to fix him a little bundle, but I didn't have much food. I usually brought our food down from the kitchen in the house. They let me have the leftovers and the things that were getting old. But I gave Hubert what I had, and I told him to follow the North Star until he got to Canada. We stood in the field in the middle of the night, trying to find the North Star. We promised each other we would be together again in Canada. And then he had to leave.

"The next morning, the foreman came to find Hubert to take him to meet the new owner. But Hubert was gone. The foreman was so angry! I knew he would be; he's an angry man most of the time. He must have asked me a hundred times where Hubert had gone, but I didn't tell him. How could I tell him? I didn't know myself. We didn't have time to make a plan. All we knew was that he had to go north, all the way to Canada. I had heard the master talking about the fugitive slave law of 1850 that says that slaves are not free if they reach the North. So I knew Hubert had to go all the way to Canada."

Tillie sniffled and blew her nose. Tina wanted to do the same and groped in her skirt pocket for a handkerchief. Mrs. Henry and Sarah sat silently. They had heard the story before.

Tillie continued.

"The foreman took me out to the tree behind the slave quarters, tied me to it, and beat me. I'd never been beaten before. I remembered that when I was a little girl, my father had been beaten twice for challenging the authority of the foreman. What the foreman was doing was costing the master a lot of money. My father had a better idea. But that did not matter. Daddy had overstepped his position as a slave, so he was beaten.

"The foreman had no mercy on me. I thought about telling him about the baby, so maybe he would feel a responsibility to protect the master's future property. But I didn't want my baby to be property! I didn't think of my baby that way."

Tillie swallowed hard, choking back tears. "I lost the baby, of course," she said so quietly that Tina almost didn't hear her.

"Tillie, I'm so sorry," Tina said. "I'm so sorry, so sorry." She did not know what else to say.

Tillie blew out a heavy breath and went on. "When I recovered and was back to working in the house, I decided to run away, too. My only chance of being with Hubert was to find him in Canada. I should have left with him. But we were afraid that my being with child would make the journey too hard. And I didn't want to slow him down."

"But now, the baby was gone. I was healthy again and fit enough to travel. I found a book about stars in the master's library and borrowed it. He had so many books, he would never miss it, I was sure. I would only need it for a few days. I read everything I could about the North Star and how to follow it. In the middle of the night, when everyone else was sleeping, I would go out into the field where I had said good-bye to Hubert, and I would look at the star and pray for him. I always hoped he was looking at the same star at the same time.

"I didn't go right away. I put the book back and started saving food—crusts of bread, pieces of dried meat, potatoes. I couldn't take much, I knew. I could only take what I could carry, and my load had to be light enough to run if I had to. But I saved what food I could. One night I said good-bye to my mama and daddy, and I left.

"Traveling in the daytime was far too dangerous. Even traveling at night was dangerous. If the moon was full, I stayed hidden. I waited for the half moon or quarter moon or for cloudy nights. I always went north. During the day, I hid wherever I could. Sometimes, I was deep in a forest, and I was not sure which way was north. Sometimes I would come across an empty shed or an old barn, and I would actually have shelter for a day or two. Of course, I was too frightened to sleep. I tried to stay awake as much as I could. But the human body needs sleep. And sometimes I would sleep for two days straight, after not sleeping for most of a week.

"The food ran out, of course. I had to start looking for berries and roots. I even stole vegetables off the back of a cart a few times. I knew I had to keep my strength up if I was going to make it to Canada.

"Finally I got to Kentucky. I took the risk of moving around in the day a few times to try to find out some information. I lingered around the docks until I figured out which boats were going to Cincinnati. I knew that if I could get to Cincinnati, I would be in free territory. One night I sneaked onto a boat that was due to go across the river the next morning. I hid in the cargo hold. I was sure no one had seen me.

"The next day, though, a boat hand came to the cargo hold and walked straight toward me. He had to have seen me get on. There was no other way he would have known where to find me. I thought I had lost everything—my chance to find Hubert, my own freedom! He would send me back to my master for sure.

"But he didn't. He did not even suggest that I should go back. He did not even ask what I was doing in the cargo hold of that boat. Instead, he told me about someone named Uncle Levi and Aunt Katy and said they would help me when I got to Cincinnati."

"Uncle Levi and Aunt Katy?" Tina asked, looking from Sarah to Mrs. Henry. "Are they relatives of yours?"

"They are in our circle of friends," Mrs. Henry said. "Levi and Katherine Coffin. Perhaps you know their shop in town."

"Yes, I think so!" Tina said. "It's one of the stores that sells goods made by free blacks, nothing made by slaves."

"That's correct," Mrs. Henry said. "Friend Levi is a conductor on the Underground Railroad. Some call him the president of the Underground Railroad. We have taken passengers for him before. But our house was searched a few months ago, and we have been overly cautious since then."

"Does Tillie have to stay scrunched up in the wall all the time?" Tina asked.

"Tillie is not actually in the wall," Mrs. Henry explained. "The false back of the cabinet leads to a room. It is hardly more than a closet. But it has a bed and a table. Tillie comes out when it is dark. But she must always stay in this room, ready to go back through the cabinet at the sound of a carriage or a knock on the door."

"When I invited thee for a visit," Sarah said, "I thought we would have no passengers. We have not had any for quite some time."

"Friend Levi is very persuasive, though," Mrs. Henry said. "He made the need for Tillie's safety quite clear. She will be with us until he is able to arrange safe passage to Canada."

"Thou must be silent about this," Sarah said quite sternly to Tina. "No one must know of thy discovery."

"I would never do anything that would put Tillie in danger," Tina said emphatically.

"Thou must be careful of thine own safety as well," Mrs. Henry said. "If anyone should learn that thou hast met Tillie, thou might be in danger."

"I won't tell anyone. I promise."

"We don't always hear the stories of our passengers," Mrs. Henry explained. "It is too dangerous for us to have that information. It is better to be able to face the authorities and honestly say we know nothing of a maid from Georgia. But Tillie told us her story in the hope that we would have news of Hubert."

"And did you?" Tina asked eagerly.

Sarah and her mother shook their heads. "He did not come through this station, nor any in Cincinnati."

"I won't tell anyone. I promise," Tina repeated.

"We must get thee home," Mrs. Henry said. "Thy visit has lasted longer than thou didst plan. Thy mother will begin to worry."

"Yes, I should go," Tina agreed. "It's late."

"Sarah will drive thee in the wagon."

CHAPTER 8
The Hidden Book

Tina turned over and punched her pillow one more time. One stubborn lump simply would not go away. Why had it never bothered her before? she wondered. She had been lying in bed for at least two hours and still had not slept for even one minute. Tina hardly ever had trouble sleeping. She hated it when she did. The more she tried to sleep, the more she couldn't. She flung her hands up over her head in frustration.

A moment later Tina got up. The room was too hot to sleep, she decided. She wanted to sit by the window and hope for at least the hint of a breeze. The air was heavy with the threat of a late summer thunderstorm. A soaking rain might cool off the air so she could sleep. But for now, the humidity drenched her nightgown. She wore the thinnest nightclothes she owned, but still she was hot and restless.

Tina moved to the window and pushed it open a little higher. She scooted a hardwood chair across the floor so she could sit with her elbows and her head leaning out the window. The outside air was not much cooler than the inside air, but at least she could feel the air move a little bit.

When she'd gotten home from Sarah's, Charles had peppered her with questions about what she had done all afternoon. She could not tell her family much about her outing. She had given her word. But Charles was persistent, as usual. Finally, Tina excused herself from supper after eating only a few bites. Claiming that she did not feel well—which she did not, because her stomach was churning—she retreated to her room.

She had given her word not to tell anyone about Tillie. She was afraid that if she spent the evening with her parents, she would be tempted to break her promise. In her room she could think her own thoughts without having to explain herself to anyone. She did not have to worry about the expression on her face or focus on the trivial questions the twins were asking.

When darkness fell, she got ready for bed and lay in the darkness waiting for the sleep that did not come.

Tina's window faced out over the front of the house. Her parents were on the porch below Tina's window, along with Uncle Tim and Uncle Ben. Charles and the twins were in bed, too, no doubt sleeping soundly, while Tina looked down on the adults below her. Leaning out the window above them, Tina could hear their conversation clearly.

"Have you decided whether to go to that meeting next week?" Mama asked her brother. "Surely the other abolitionist lawyers can meet without you one time." Mama sat in a wicker chair, while Uncle Tim was perched on the porch railing.

"But what about the next time?" Uncle Tim answered. "If I let them scare me away from this meeting, they'll try something else the next time." He slapped the railing. "Free speech is a founding principle of this country. I have every right to go to that meeting!"

"Of course you do," Papa agreed quickly. "But should you? That is a separate question."

"Have you told the authorities about the threatening letter?" Uncle Ben asked.

Uncle Tim nodded. "They offer little help. Unless someone actually hurts the children, they cannot do much—especially since I don't know who sent the letter. I have my suspicions, but no proof."

"Perhaps you should pull out of the Railroad for a while," Papa said, "just for a few weeks or a few months. Let these pro-slavery people focus on someone else for a while."

"I have no wish to put someone else in danger," Uncle Tim said quickly. "There are some good folks working as conductors and station managers, especially the Quakers. I will not put them at risk."

"And what about Daniel and Elise?" Mama asked quietly.

"They are safe. Dot can see them nearly every day." He

paused and looked up at the night sky. "They will come home. This is a test. When I have passed the test, the children will come home."

"I pray for them every night—and for you," Mama said.

Uncle Tim smiled. "I'm sure your prayers are one of the reasons I feel certain the children are safe."

"So you will go to the meeting on Friday?" Papa asked.

"I must."

Tina pulled her head back inside the room. She had been surprised that afternoon to discover that Rebecca Henry knew Uncle Tim. Was Uncle Tim himself a conductor on the Underground Railroad? she wondered. Did he harbor runaway slaves at his house and help them get to Canada? He took trips sometimes—he called them business trips. Now Tina wondered what business he meant.

Tina lay on her bed once again with her eyes wide open. She could not get the picture of Tillie out of her mind. Tillie huddling in the secret compartment in a wall behind a cabinet. Tillie wearing a dress that Tina recognized as Sarah's, because she had no clothes of her own anymore. Tillie bearing the grief of her lost child and the pain of not knowing where her husband was—or whether he was still alive. Tillie stealing food to stay alive.

Why did I have to get so snoopy? Tina asked herself. *If I had minded my own business and stayed out of that cabinet, I wouldn't know anything about this. Sarah and I would have had a nice afternoon together, and I wouldn't be hiding a secret from my family.*

But she did know about Tillie, and she did have a secret. Tina remembered her uncle's words, "This is a test."

In the dark, alone, she shook her head from side to side. *I promised not to say anything to anyone, and I won't,* she thought. *But that's the end of it. Mrs. Henry will take good care of Tillie. I can only pray that someday she finds Hubert, and they will have a whole bunch of babies born in freedom.*

Tina whispered a prayer for Tillie and Hubert right then. She felt better, but still she could not sleep. She was too worried, too confused, and too hot.

She sat up again, and this time she reached for the candle on the table next to her bed. She lit it quickly. The steadily murmuring voices of her parents and uncles out on the porch made her sure she could do what she planned to do.

Crouching next to her bed, she slid her hand under the mattress. What she was looking for was not there. She propped the mattress on her shoulder and reached in farther until she found it. Slowly Tina pulled out her hand. In her hands she held a book. The candle cast its glow across the title: *Uncle Tom's Cabin,* by Harriet Beecher Stowe.

The book belonged to Uncle Tim, but he did not know Tina had it—another secret from her family. Uncle Tim had purchased the book and read it as soon as it was published two years earlier, in 1852. For weeks he had talked about nothing else but *Uncle Tom's Cabin* and the stories that Harriet Beecher Stowe told about the mistreatment of slaves. Mrs. Stowe lived in Ohio and knew Cincinnati well. Uncle Tim was convinced that she had used real stories of runaways to form the characters in her book. He thought it was a wonderful book.

But not everyone agreed with Uncle Tim. Many people in the South wanted the book banned. That opinion only made Uncle Tim like it even more. And it made Tina all the more curious. One day, while visiting Uncle Tim's law office, she had noticed the book tucked in between his legal volumes.

Tina was certain he was finished with the book and would not miss it if she borrowed it. But she was too timid to ask Uncle Tim if she could borrow it. He would get excited about her interest in the abolitionist cause. He would never understand that she was simply curious about the book. So, with her heart beating so fast she could hardly breathe, she had borrowed it anyway. But she never told anyone she had done so. She was not sure she wanted anyone to know she was reading such a controversial book.

Tina pulled the candle closer to the edge of the nightstand and tried to get comfortable in her bed. She opened up the book and began to read: "Chapter 1: In Which the Reader is Introduced to a Man of Humanity. Late in the afternoon of a chilly day in February. . ."

The more she read, the less tired Tina felt—and the less she noticed the heat and humidity. Harriet Beecher Stowe's characters captured her complete attention. When she read of how the young mother Eliza crossed the Ohio River on ice blocks, carrying her baby in her arms, tears sprang to Tina's eyes. Had Tillie's baby lived, that could have been Tillie making such a brave escape.

Were slave catchers chasing Tillie, she wondered, the way they had chased Eliza in the book? Tillie had left

Georgia months ago. Perhaps her owners had stopped looking for her. But she could never be sure, Tina knew. She could never be free until she crossed the border into Canada.

Tina laid the book in her lap to ponder the story for a few minutes. Suddenly she heard footsteps on the stairs. She had not even heard her uncles leave and her parents come into the house. A glance at the candle, now much lower and dimmer than when she pulled out the book, told her that she had been reading for a long time.

Her parents would have expected her to be asleep a long time ago, especially if she was not feeling well, as she had claimed at suppertime. Reluctantly, Tina blew out the candle and laid back down in her bed. She punched at the knot in the pillow once more.

Lying in the dark, Tina thought that she had not pondered the subject of bravery in her whole life as much as she had in one day: Uncle Tim, Tillie, even fictional characters in the book. Tina admired them all. But could she ever be like them?

CHAPTER 9

The Slave Catcher

Four days later, Tina was finally starting to feel like herself. School on Thursday and Friday had given her something to concentrate on. On Saturday, she spent the afternoon with the twins, and her cousin Meg had come by to make plans for their carriage ride. They would go on Sunday afternoon, after the big dinner that Tina's mother always made after church.

On Sunday morning, Tina dressed for church in her Sunday dress—a pink printed bodice with tiny green buds and a dark pink hooped skirt. Her red hair had a mind of its own, but on Sundays Tina always made a special effort to control it. A bow that matched her dress kept her hair pulled back from her face, allowing her green eyes to shine.

Pamela Fisk insisted that the family eat breakfast together on Sunday mornings. The kitchen still smelled like pancakes and sausage when Tina came downstairs again, dressed for church. In the heavy iron frying pan on the stove was one last, unclaimed sausage. Careful not to drip grease on her skirt, Tina delicately picked it up between her fingers and took a bite. It was pork sausage. She was surprised Charles had not devoured every last crumb long ago.

Tina glanced at a clock and decided she had time to look at a newspaper before leaving for church. Her father always read it first thing in the morning and left the paper neatly folded, just the way he found it. Tina was careful not to disturb the order of the pages as she unfolded the paper and started looking through the headlines.

The main topics were always the same, she noticed. The Republican Party, which had been organized in Ohio earlier in the year, was becoming more active. She scanned an article that predicted the Republicans would be successful in getting their candidate elected as president of the United States within a few years.

Kansas and Nebraska were still debating whether to allow slavery in their territories. Nearly every week the paper carried a story of a violent outbreak in either Kansas or Nebraska. Abolitionists, like her uncle Tim, wrote editorials criticizing anyone who defended the rights of the Southern states to continue the system of slavery if they chose to.

Tina turned to a section of the newspaper she did not

usually look at: advertisements. But she was not looking for furniture or clothing. She quickly found the page that contained classified advertisements offering rewards for helping to find runaway slaves. She read each one carefully.

"Reward: Two hundred dollars for capture of Isaac, Alabama slave. Strong, muscular build, six feet tall, very dark color. Scar on left cheek. Valuable property."

"Runaway slaves posing as free negresses available for hire. Last seen wearing women's clothing. Slight of build. One speaks with lisp. Owner offers handsome reward for return in good health."

"Light-skinned negro perhaps passing as white. Young man, small of build but quite strong. Last seen in Kentucky, south of Cincinnati. Worth $1,100. Owner offering $300 for capture and return."

"Young negress, nineteen years old. Unusually refined bearing and language. Well educated. Escaped from Georgia plantation. May try to hire out as qualified household help. Owner offering reward for information leading to capture."

Tina's heart nearly stopped. She reread the last advertisement carefully, word for word. Tillie! This was an exact description of everything Tina knew about Tillie. *Had the ad run before?* Tina wondered. And had Sarah's family seen it? Did they know a slave catcher was in town looking for Tillie?

"Hey, who ate the last pork sausage?" Charles demanded as he swung open the kitchen door and inspected the pan. "I was going to come back for that."

Tina winced at the accusation. "Sorry. I didn't think anyone wanted it. It was cold."

"I like them cold or hot. You know that."

"Sorry," Tina repeated.

Charles sank into a chair next to her. "Next time you see a sausage left over, call me!" He glanced at the newspaper lying open on the table. "Why are you reading the ads for runaway slaves?"

Tina closed the paper quickly. "I was just flipping through the paper, like I always do. You should try it sometime. You might learn a thing or two."

"I can find out everything I need to know without reading a silly newspaper," Charles said. "For instance, I know who the slave catcher is who placed those ads."

Tina felt the color drain from her face. "You do?"

"Sure. He comes through the train station all the time. He makes regular visits to the Northern cities looking for slaves. If you help him find one, he gives you part of the reward, but he gets most of it."

"How do you know all this?" Tina asked, still skeptical.

"I told you, he comes through the station all the time. He tried to hire me to carry his bags one time."

"Did you do it?"

"Naw. I didn't want to help any slave catcher. He can do his own work."

"Did you really meet him?"

"Why don't you ever believe anything I tell you? I met him. His name is Kenyon LeClaire. He's very tall, taller than Papa, and he wears black suits with different colored waistcoats. He has a pocket watch he likes to check. It's on a gold chain. He carries a cane, but I don't think he really needs it. He just thinks it looks fancy."

"That doesn't sound much like a slave catcher," Tina said doubtfully.

"How many slave catchers have you actually known?" Charles challenged.

"Well, none, but you just described a very proper gentleman. Slave catchers are nasty people who will do anything for money."

"He's a Southern gentleman," Charles said. "A Southern gentleman can be a slave catcher. Remember, slaves are property, not people. Believe me, Kenyon LeClaire is hunting for escaped slaves."

Tina was becoming convinced that her brother did know this slave catcher.

"Is he in town now?" Tina asked. "Have you seen him lately?"

"He got here on the afternoon train yesterday," Charles answered. "I saw him coming and cleared out of there before he tried to hire me again."

The door from the dining room swung open, and Mama stuck her head in. "There you are, you two. The twins are ready at last. Let's go before David starts taking his clothes off and throwing them in the street."

"Tina ate the last sausage, Mama. I was coming back for it," Charles whined. "I told you I wanted it, but you said I had to go get dressed."

"Don't start on that," his mother warned. "You're far too old to be squabbling about cold sausage. Now let's go. Your father is bringing the carriage around."

When they pulled up in front of the church, David still had his clothes on, but he had made several attempts to remove his shirt. Tina's neatly placed bow was cockeyed because of her efforts to keep her small brother suitably dressed. She was relieved to get out of the carriage and set David on the ground. Squealing, he ran across the church lawn toward the door. Tina's father chased him with as much dignity as possible and scooped up David just before the boy collided with the oldest member of the congregation.

Tina followed with her mother, who had a firm grip on Daria's hand. Charles lingered behind but eventually came in and sat next to Tina in the family pew. The twins were squeezed in on either side of their father, trapped so they could not escape and trample the feet of the congregation.

Tina was determined to pay particular attention to the service that morning. She had tried to pray for Tillie in the last four days, but she thought she might concentrate better on praying if she was in church instead of her bedroom. She looked up the number of the first hymn, found the page, and sat ready to sing. The organ swelled with the introduction, the pastor gestured that the congregation should stand, and Tina did. Her voice was not strong in the midst of the congregation, but she sang earnestly and accurately.

After an invocation and another hymn, the pastor began to pray. Tina squeezed her eyes shut and concentrated on his words: "Oh, Father in Heaven, we bow before Thee, humble creatures who know Thy will and do not do it, who hear Thy voice and do not answer. Imbue us with Thy Spirit that we may obediently answer Thy call."

A poke in the ribs nearly made Tina cry out in the

middle of the prayer. She opened one eye and peeked at Charles. He tilted his head toward the center aisle. Tina glanced across the center aisle but saw nothing special. She opened both eyes and scowled at Charles. Her parents had their heads bowed. Even the twins sat with their hands folded and their eyes squeezed shut. What was Charles up to?

He tilted his head again. Still Tina saw nothing unusual. She shrugged her shoulders at Charles. Then his lips began moving. Carefully and silently they formed the words "slave catcher."

Tina looked across the aisle once more. Sure enough, across the aisle, two rows ahead of her in the middle of the pew sat a man who fit Charles's description of the slave catcher perfectly. Even though the man was seated, Tina could see that he was unusually tall. He wore a black morning coat with soft gray trim. As Tina watched, he reached into a pocket in his red waistcoat and pulled out his gold watch. He looked at it, snapped it shut, and tucked it away again. His other hand rested atop a polished cane he help upright in front of him.

Tina was convinced that Charles had not made up Kenyon LeClaire. His description had been perfect. But how did Charles know Kenyon LeClaire was a slave catcher?

The pastor finished praying and began his sermon. Tina resolved to pay attention. If she listened hard enough, maybe she could make sense of everything that had happened during the last few days. But her mind wandered anyway. Every few minutes she looked over at Kenyon LeClaire. Almost every time she looked at him, he was checking his watch. Charles had been right about that, too.

What was a slave catcher doing in church? Tina wondered. Kenyon LeClaire looked comfortable in the church service. He seemed to know the hymns that they sang and the prayers they spoke. Except for checking his watch, he paid rapt attention to the pastor—better than Tina was doing, she thought guiltily.

Charles nudged her again. It was time to stand and sing the last hymn. He found the page and handed her the book.

"Stop daydreaming," Charles whispered harshly as the hymn began.

Tina sighed and tried to sing. The hymn was familiar. She could sing it without thinking. She looked across the aisle again. Kenyon LeClaire did not have his hymnal open, yet he sang energetically and confidently.

Finally Tina decided that Kenyon LeClaire went to church every Sunday. He probably had a regular pew that he sat in with his family somewhere in the South. He knew the hymns because he had been singing them all his life, just as she had. Uncle Tim thought slavery was evil. People like Kenyon LeClaire just thought it was a good way to make money and support their families.

The hymn ended, and the pastor began the benediction. Frustrated that she had let herself be sidetracked for most of the service, Tina offered up a quick prayer for Tillie's safety and for Uncle Tim's decision.

At the pastor's *Amen*, the twins nearly knocked Tina over as they scrambled to get out of the pew.

CHAPTER 10
Caught!

The twins hardly touched their food at Sunday dinner—except the bread, of course. Charles had three helpings of ham and two baked potatoes. Tina had especially enjoyed the peas and green beans from the Fisk garden. The entire family had eaten heartily of one thing or another. Still, there was a lot of food left over.

Tina scraped and stacked the plates and carried them into the kitchen. Her mother was filling the sink with hot water from the stove to begin washing. The kitchen was strewn with her efforts to give her family a formal Sunday dinner with everything from ham to two kinds of pies.

"Mama, there is too much food left over," Tina said. "We'll never be able to keep it fresh enough to eat again."

"I wouldn't worry," Mama said. "Charles will come through in about two hours and have more of everything. I'll be surprised if there is anything left by tomorrow at lunchtime."

Tina was still skeptical. She examined the platters of food waiting to be put away. It still looked like an awful lot to her: half a ham, eight baked potatoes, two loaves of bread her mother had baked just last night, a bowl of apples from the backyard tree, vegetables from the garden. She nibbled at a green bean.

A crash sounded from the living room, followed by a double wail. Mama rolled her eyes. "I was hoping they could sit quietly just long enough to get the kitchen cleaned up."

The wailing got louder.

"Mama, she hit me!"

"He hit me first!"

"She took my toy!"

"It was my toy first!"

Mama pulled her hands out of the dishwater and dried them on her apron.

"Your father had an emergency and had to go to the clinic," she said, "and, of course, Charles is gone."

"To the train station?"

"Where else?"

"Don't worry, Mama," Tina said. "I'll clean up what I can."

"Wouldn't it be wonderful if I could get them to take a nap today?"

Tina smiled. "So you could have a nap, too? Go ahead, Mama. Try. Don't worry about this mess."

Before that day, Tina had never wondered much about what Charles did at the train station all the time. Now she did.

Tina decided to start with the leftover food, beginning with the ham. She took the cleaver firmly in her right hand and began slicing off chunks of meat. If Charles really was going to come looking for more food in two hours, it might as well be ready for him. The ham had been salted and preserved for months. It would keep well. Her mother would probably put the vegetables out again at suppertime, but Tina was sure there would still be some left over. It was that time of year, when the garden yielded its abundance and the family feasted on fresh food.

Tina spied a basket at one end of the work counter. It was a large one she had not seen her mother use for a long time. At first, Tina wondered why it was out. Then she had an idea of her own. She knew someone who needed all this food more than her family did. Tina knew that she would have to explain to her mother—and probably Charles—where the leftover food had gone. She decided to leave half of the food for her family and wrap up the other half.

Tillie's thin face floated before Tina's eyes. She knew the food would be used well and wisely. Her hands worked faster and faster. But the basket was a deep one. Even with several thick slices of ham and a loaf of bread, along with vegetables and apples, there was a lot of space left.

She would fill up the space. That was all there was to it. First Tina took a minute to peek through the door and see what her mother was doing. She did not find her mother or the twins in sight. And she heard no more noises from the living room. *She's taken them upstairs,* Tina thought. *They've probably all fallen asleep.*

Her mother's pantry was well stocked. It would be easy to take a few items that would never be missed: a sack of flour, some fruit preserves, a bag of rice, some dried beans. Soon the basket was full—and it was heavy. Now Tina was beginning to think she had a problem. How would she get the basket out of the house and over to Sarah's house? Certainly she could not carry this load for an hour's walk.

Then she remembered Meg. This was the day of their carriage ride into the country. All Tina had to do was persuade Meg to drive out Deer Creek Road in the direction of the Henry farm. She added enough extra ham and bread for a small picnic and tucked in a tablecloth and two napkins. Tina set the basket outside the back door, where it would be out of sight for a few minutes.

With the food put away, Tina plunged into the task of cleaning the dishes. She scrubbed the plates rapidly and then attacked the pots and pans. Finally she was ready to take a rag and wipe down the sideboard and kitchen table.

Meg knocked on the front door just as Tina hung her apron on its hook.

"Ready?" Meg said brightly. "I've got my father's best carriage. We'll travel in style today."

"Wonderful," Tina responded, opening the door and

welcoming her cousin. "I'll be ready in just a moment."

"It's too quiet around here," Meg commented. "Where is everyone?"

"Either out or asleep, I think," Tina murmured in response. She was glad the rest of her family were not around. Their absence would make her task easier. "I packed us a basket in case we get hungry later."

Meg smiled. "If Sunday dinner at your house is anything like it is at mine, you're stuffed right now."

"Yes," Tina agreed. "But that could change, you know. I want to be prepared. I'll just get the basket and take it out to the carriage. If you want to say hello to my mother, I think she's upstairs with the twins. You could get a quilt from my room while you're up there."

"I'll just take a quick peek," Meg said, "and meet you at the carriage. It's right out front."

Tina breathed a sigh of relief. This was going to be easier than she thought—at least the first stage. She was pretty sure her mother was asleep and Meg would return in a minute. She had to move quickly. Careful not to let the back door slam, Tina went out, retrieved her basket, and carried it around to the front of the house. It fit neatly under the seat of the carriage.

Tina had just climbed into the carriage when Meg returned.

"You were right," she said. "They were all asleep." She handed a quilt up to Tina.

"I hope they stay that way for a while," Tina said. "Mama could use the extra rest."

"Where shall we go?" Meg asked.

Tina could not believe her good fortune. She was going to get to suggest the route.

"When I was at my friend Sarah's the other day, I noticed a lovely spot for a picnic."

"But we just ate, Tina. Why don't we just drive a bit farther?"

Tina shrugged. "Even if we don't eat, it looked like a nice place to relax. It was grassy and shaded and away from the city."

"Sounds wonderful. Let's go."

"Just head out Deer Creek Road." Tina sighed in relief.

Meg clicked her tongue and the horse responded appropriately, trotting gently down the street that would take them out of the city.

"Sarah is a Quaker, isn't she?" Meg asked.

"Yes," Tina answered cautiously.

"How did you two become friends? It doesn't seem that you have much in common."

"Sarah's mother was sick a couple years ago—a bad fever and chills. Papa helped her. I met Sarah when she brought her mother to the clinic."

"Your father has a wonderful clinic," Meg said. She seemed to have lost interest in Sarah. "I'm hoping that some day he will let me work as a nurse in his practice full time."

"I didn't know you wanted to do that. I always thought you were planning to go to California."

A dark expression passed over Meg's face, and she stared straight ahead. When she spoke, her voice was hardly more than a whisper. "I used to think that. I was waiting for Damon Pollard to come back for me. We were going to build a life together in California. But he's gone now. The accident that killed him ended that part of my life. Now I have something else to focus on."

"Medicine?"

"That's right. Between your father and cousin Henry Lankford I'm trying to learn as much as I can."

Before long they neared the turnoff to go toward Sarah's house. While they chattered, Tina's mind was planning how she was going to be able to slip away from Meg for a few minutes. In the meantime, she wanted to keep Meg talking.

"What if you meet someone else and get married?" Tina asked. "Would you still be a nurse?"

Meg shook her head vigorously. "I'll never get married. I was lucky to have Damon, but there won't be anybody else like him."

"I know enough about my father's work to know that being a nurse will not be easy."

"I know it will be a challenge," Meg said. "But I'm ready to accept the challenge. If I'm a nurse, I can help people who are really hurting—people who might not otherwise get medical care."

"Like people in the German section, where your grandparents used to live?" Tina asked. "I remember that you used to go there a lot."

"I still do."

Tina pointed to a road veering to the left. "That's the turnoff. We're getting close."

"We haven't really driven very far, and we're having

such a nice conversation," Meg said. "Are you sure you want to stop here?"

Tina's heart pounded. "Yes, please, let's do stop. It's such a lovely spot. You must see it. We can keep talking there."

"Of course, if you think the spot is perfect, then that's where we'll go."

Without further protest, Meg guided the horse to make the turn and they trotted down the lane. Their conversation lagged. Once again, Tina struggled mentally for a plan that would give her a few minutes alone. If only she could confide in Meg! This task would be so much easier, and she was sure Meg would understand. But she had given her word not to tell anyone.

"You're right," Meg said pleasantly. "This is a lovely lane."

Tina judged that it would take about five minutes to walk to Sarah's house from anywhere along this lane, less if she hurried.

"Pick a spot you like," Tina suggested.

Meg abruptly stopped the horse. "Look! Wildflowers! They're beautiful. Usually they are all gone by this time in September."

Before them spread a field of green grass growing uncut, dappled with bold sunflowers, lacey white blooms, and vibrant purples. It was a beautiful sight, Tina agreed. She remembered that she had noticed it on her Wednesday visit to Sarah. But her encounter with Tillie had blurred her memory of anything else that happened that day.

Meg guided the horse to the side of the lane and

hopped out of the carriage. "Let's go look!" Meg said. "I think I see a salsify patch. That's my favorite."

Tina smiled at her cousin's unexpected youthful enthusiasm. "You go ahead," Tina said. "I'll spread out the blanket and make sure the carriage is taken care of. I'll catch up with you."

"I only wish I'd brought my paints and a canvas. It would be wonderful to capture those colors so I could look at them whenever I wanted."

"I didn't know you still painted, since you started studying medicine."

"I will always paint," Meg declared. She crossed the road, mesmerized, and wandered out into the field.

Tina worked quickly. First she made sure the horse was tied to a tree so he couldn't wander off. Quickly she spread the blanket in a grassy spot. She pulled the basket out from under the seat. Then she looked around to get her bearings and started in the direction of Sarah's house.

She was right. It took her only a few minutes to get to the house. She planned to empty the basket on the steps leading up the side of the porch, where the food would be in the shade. Someone would find the food and know what it was for. There was no need to prolong her visit to the Henry house.

As she began unloading the basket, Tina glanced around. No one was in sight. She knew she had only a few minutes before Meg would be expecting her.

As she took out the last jar of preserves and set it on the step, someone reached from behind her and clamped a hand down on her wrist.

CHAPTER 11
A Mission for the Railroad

Tina gasped. With as much force as she could muster, she yanked herself out of the hold of the strange hand. She rolled over and started kicking the air in self-defense.

Then she saw the face.

"Sarah! You scared me half to death. What in the world are you doing?"

"What art thou doing?" Sarah countered.

Tina stood up and brushed off her skirt, then gestured

to the items she had left on the steps. “I brought food. I thought you could use it. . .you know.”

“Yes, I know, and if thou leavest a pile of strange food on our doorstep, anyone passing by will know.”

Tina looked at the ground. “I didn’t think about that. I figured you would find it right away. Besides,” she said, lifting her head, “no one just passes by your house. You are not exactly on the main street of Cincinnati.”

“Thou art right. I am sorry.”

Tina glanced down the lane. She had not planned to get caught up in a conversation. Meg would soon wonder where she was. Perhaps another minute would not matter.

“How is Tillie?” she asked.

“She is gaining strength every day,” Sarah answered. “Soon she will be strong enough to continue the journey.”

Tina nodded, satisfied. “That’s good. Then she’ll need what I brought.”

Sarah sat on a step and considered Tina carefully. “Thou hast done a kind thing,” she said, “and my mother will appreciate the gesture as well. Does thee want to help—really help?”

“I. . .what do you mean? Didn’t I help by bringing food?” She glanced down the lane toward Meg once again.

“Tillie needs something else that thou couldst give.”

“What do you mean?”

“There is a slave catcher in town looking for Tillie.”

“I know. But I didn’t know that you knew.”

“The information that comes to us is quite reliable,” Sarah said. “Tillie will need some extra help. She is much too refined.” Sarah chuckled ever so slightly. “My mother is teaching her to slouch. She has become quite good at it. And she is practicing slang."

"I still don't understand what you are talking about," Tina said.

"Tillie must leave Cincinnati with another identity—that of a teenage boy. She has a boyish build, but she is not overly tall."

"What are you asking me for?"

"Some clothes."

"Clothes? For a teenage boy?"

Sarah nodded. "Thy brother is tall for his age—taller than thee. His clothes would fit Tillie well."

"I thought there were sewing circles that made clothes for the Underground Railroad. I'm sure I've heard my uncle say that.

" 'Tis true," Sarah said, "but we don't have enough things for children right now. And Tillie might have to leave before the next delivery. Wilt thou help?"

Tina backed up a few steps. "I don't know, Sarah. If Charles found out—or my mother—how would I explain it?"

Sarah shrugged. "I did not say it would be easy. But it is needful."

"But Charles doesn't have very many clothes. He just has a few favorite things. If I took something, he would miss it right away."

"Perhaps there is something he has outgrown, something he does not wear anymore."

Tina was silent, thinking.

"Tina, we have not much time. Tillie must be ready to travel on short notice."

Tina took a deep breath and swallowed hard. "All right. I'll do it."

Sarah grinned. "I knew thee had a good heart. Take the clothes to Levi Coffin's store on Monday. Just look around the store for a few minutes, then leave the bundle. Do not speak to anyone. Just leave the bundle and walk away."

Tina felt weak in the knees. What had she gotten herself into?

"I must go," she murmured. "My cousin is waiting for me. I have been gone too long already."

"Pray, stay one more moment," Sarah said, reaching out to grab Tina's hand. "There is one more thing."

Tina looked nervously at her friend.

"Tillie needs an escort, someone to take her to the place where she will meet the others who are making the journey."

"You want me to take Tillie somewhere?" Tina's green eyes were as wide as they had ever been.

"It is a needful thing, Tina. My parents are being watched too carefully, and Levi and Katherine Coffin are well known also. But no one would suspect thee. If thou wast driving a wagon, no one would stop thee."

"It still sounds dangerous to me," Tina said.

"Thou couldst accomplish this task after school and still be home for supper," Sarah said.

Tears welled up in Tina's eyes. "I want to help, Sarah, I really do. But I don't think I could do what you are asking. I would be responsible for Tillie's safety, all on my own. What if I did something that was dangerous for her?"

"Thou wouldst only follow a plan laid out by someone else."

"But something could go wrong, and then I would not know what to do." Tina shook her head adamantly and wiped the tears from her cheeks with the back of her hand. "No, Sarah, I can't do that. I'll get the clothes and take them to Coffin's, but that's all."

Then Tina turned and ran before Sarah could say anything more.

Back at the carriage a few minutes later, Tina slid the almost empty basket back under the seat. She scanned the field for Meg, who was about fifty yards away, walking among the sunflowers. Tina did not feel ready to face Meg. Instead, she buried her head in the horse's mane and let the tears come once again. But she did not indulge herself for long.

Tina straightened her skirt, smoothed back her hair, wiped her eyes, and looked around. She started walking toward her cousin. It was important to look normal, to convince Meg that she was enjoying an afternoon out. Tina breathed deeply in and out several times.

"There you are," Meg said brightly when Tina approached her. "I was beginning to think you had decided to take a nap on that blanket instead of coming out here."

Tina smiled weakly. "It was tempting."

"I'm finding all sorts of interesting things," Meg said. "Some of these things are weeds, I'm sure, but they are exquisite. Look at these." She leaned over and cupped a blossom in her hand. "This is fireweed. I see at least four shades of pink on one petal. Do you see that?"

Tina nodded, but did not speak.

"Over there," Meg said, pointing, "I saw white sweet

clover. The flowers are like little peas. Did you smell them? They smell like new-mown hay."

Once again, Tina nodded.

Meg stopped and looked at Tina's face. "Are you all right, Tina? You look flushed."

Tina put her hands to her cheeks. "It must be the sun and the effort of walking through this high field."

"If you're not feeling well, we can go back."

"No, I feel fine!" Tina asserted. "I don't want to spoil the afternoon."

This would be a perfect time to confide in Meg, Tina thought. No one could possibly hear what they said to each other out here. Anyone passing by would simply see a girl and a young woman walking through a field on a pleasant Sunday afternoon. Meg would be able to help her sort out all the questions in her mind. Tina came very close to speaking Meg's name.

"Shall we take a bouquet back for your mother?" Meg suggested.

"Oh yes, she would like that." Tina laughed. "Of course, the twins will have the flowers strewn all over the house within ten minutes."

"We shall make sure that they don't," Meg said. "I want your mother to have these."

"You sound determined."

"I am." Meg bent over and snapped off a stem of fireweed. "If I really want something, I'll work to make it happen."

"Like being a nurse?" Tina asked.

"We've moved rather quickly from flowers to medicine,"

Meg observed, taking a moment to catch Tina's eye.

"Keeping the twins away from the flowers will be easy compared to becoming a nurse," Tina said. "Do you think you really will become a nurse?"

Meg nodded. "With God's help, I will." She snapped another flower.

Meg's phrase rang in Tina's mind: *With God's help, I will.* She said, "I think you're very brave to try something like that."

"Oh, I'm not sure bravery has much to do with it," Meg said as she buried her nose in her handful of flowers. "There's something inside me telling me that I must do this."

"So you're not afraid of how hard it might be?"

Meg tilted her head thoughtfully to one side. "I know it will be hard. But I feel it is something that I must do. So I will."

"With God's help," Tina murmured.

"That's right. With God's help." Meg raised her face to the sun. "I think you're right about the sun. I'm ready to sit in the shade for a while. What about you?"

"Sure," Tina responded, and they turned to walk back to where they had left the carriage.

Meg plopped down on the blanket. "I hope you put something to drink in that basket you packed."

"Coming right up," Tina said, and she soon produced a clay jar of cool water. They passed it back and forth and drank deeply, letting some of the water trickle across their faces.

Meg looked at the basket that now sat between them

on the blanket. "That's a big basket for a snack just for the two of us."

Tina shrugged. "It was already sitting out, so I used it instead of looking for another."

"I can't believe it," Meg said, putting one hand on her stomach, "but I am starting to feel hungry. Let's see what you've got in there."

Tina lifted the napkin that covered the basket and pulled out some bread and ham. It was all that was left. "We can make sandwiches," she said. "Oh, and I have an apple for your horse."

Tina hopped up and walked over to where the horse was casually munching grass. She patted the back of his neck with one hand while she offered the apple with the other. He took it eagerly.

While she waited for the horse to finish the apple, Tina looked down the lane toward Sarah's house.

With God's help, I will, she thought.

Chapter 12
Time for Action

Tina waved good-bye to Meg and watched as her cousin nudged the horse forward and he trotted away obediently. They had lain on the blanket, watching the clouds for a long time before deciding that they really ought to go home. Supper had come and gone by the time they got to the Fisk house.

Resting under the tree with Meg beside her, Tina had again battled the urge to tell Meg her secret. Meg would understand. She might even help. But Tina kept her promise.

Instead of talking about Tillie, she told funny stories about the twins. It felt good to laugh. Still, Tillie never left Tina's mind all afternoon. What if she had said yes to Sarah's request? Should she have said yes? The most important thing was for Tillie to be safe, and Tina wasn't sure she wouldn't put Tillie in even more danger.

When the carriage was out of sight, Tina turned and walked toward the front porch of her home. Her father, her brother, and Uncle Tim sat on the porch.

"The wanderer has come home," Papa said to his daughter, smiling. "Did you have a nice day with Meg?"

"Yes, very pleasant," Tina said. She remembered the wildflowers in her hand. "We picked these for Mama."

"She'll appreciate that, I'm sure."

"Uncle Tim?" Tina asked.

"What can I do for you, Tina?" her uncle responded.

"Now that the meeting is behind you, can the children come home?"

"They can and they have," Uncle Tim declared. "First thing yesterday morning we collected them, and I must say it's good to have them home again."

"But Uncle Tim," Tina added, "is it safe for them? Couldn't the people who threatened them still try to kidnap them or worse?"

Uncle Tim frowned. "That they could, Tina. I can't deny the truth of your words. We've taken extra steps to help keep the children safe, but there are no guarantees. We can only do the best we know how. And the sooner we resolve the slavery issue, the sooner black and white children will truly be safe. It's as I was telling your papa, the Southern states must understand that the welfare of the nation comes first. Their rights are secondary."

"They don't see it that way, Tim," Papa said.

"They must see it that way! We will not stop our work until they understand—until they do away with slavery."

"Tim, you know I hate slavery as much as you do. But for a lot of people in the South, their income depends on the slaves. If they had to pay someone to do what the slaves do, they couldn't make a profit. Their own families would suffer."

"I can't believe you are defending the Southerners," Uncle Tim said gruffly. "Especially after the threats my family received."

"I am not defending them," Papa said calmly. "And I'm certainly relieved that your meeting went off without any problems. It's good that Daniel and Elise can once again be home with their parents. I pray that you will never again have to face such difficult choices."

Papa sighed. "I'm just trying to get you to understand the Southerners' point of view. You want to take away the main part of their economy, but you offer nothing in its place."

"Slavery is a moral question, not an economic question," Uncle Tim snapped. "We must do the right thing now, right now, not when it is economically convenient. It is simply not right to have slave owners coming to the North and hunting people like they were wild animals. I've known of more than one free black man who was captured and sold into slavery, even though he had been free all his life in the North."

"That is inexcusable," Papa said. "That goes far beyond the question of whether an escaped slave is someone's property or not."

Charles jumped up and swung his first in the air. "I'm not afraid of those slave catchers. I could set them straight real fast."

Uncle Tim looked somberly at Charles. "I hope that by the time you are old enough to be active in politics, the issue of slavery will be settled. We should not pass this burden on to another generation."

Uncle Tim turned back to Papa. "What disturbs me most of all is the possibility that slavery will expand into new territories. If that happens, we will surely pass this ugly thing on to our children."

"You are doing everything you can, Tim," Papa said. "And you know I would never hesitate to treat a black person who needed medical attention. You have many friends around Cincinnati who would work right alongside you."

"I would," Charles said enthusiastically, "if you would just give me a chance! Give me a job for the Underground Railroad, Uncle Tim. I'll do it. You'll see. I'm brave enough to help you."

Brave enough or foolish enough? Tina wondered.

"Shh, calm down, Charles," Papa said. "This is not a conversation that the whole neighborhood needs to hear."

Charles slumped into a chair.

"I believe I heard your mother remind you about some schoolwork to do before tomorrow morning," Papa continued, looking sternly at his son. "Is that correct?"

"Yes, sir," muttered Charles.

"Go get your books, Son. It'll be time for bed before long."

"Yes, sir." Charles dragged himself out of the chair like a floppy doll and started shuffling toward the front door.

Papa stopped him and took his son's face in his hands. Looking straight into Charles's eyes, he said, "Charles, one day you will do something great. I'm sure of that. It will be important work. But if you can't get through school, it will be a lot harder for you to do those great things. Do you understand?"

"Yes, sir."

"Good night, Son."

"Good night, Papa." Charles straightened up and went into the house.

"I have some things to do, too," Tina said.

"I thought you finished your homework already," Papa said.

"I did. I have something else I need to do. And I'd better get these flowers into some water."

"That's fine, but don't dawdle. I want you in bed on time tonight. You need a good rest."

"Yes, Papa. I won't be long."

Tina followed Charles into the house. She knew his schoolbooks were in the kitchen. He always left his satchel on the sideboard when he came home from school. From the living room, Tina could hear the sounds of Charles getting settled: the scraping of a chair on the floor as he sat down at the kitchen table, the rustling of paper as he found his page in the book.

She pushed open the kitchen door. "I just need to get a vase," she said.

"They don't take me seriously," Charles grumbled. "I want to help Uncle Tim, but he won't let me."

Tina chose her words carefully. "You'll get your chance, Charles. Just be patient." She took a vase from the cupboard and filled it with water.

"That's easy for you to say. You don't care. You would never be brave enough to work in the Underground Railroad."

Tina arranged the flowers in the vase. She kept her back to Charles so he could not see her face. If only Charles knew the truth about what she was going to do in just a few minutes.

"Do you need any help with your schoolwork?" she asked.

"Naw. I just get tired of book learning. I want to do something."

"You will," Tina said. "You will."

Charles sighed and turned a page in his book.

Satisfied that Charles was concentrating on his homework, Tina took the next step in her plan. Quietly, so that she would not draw attention to herself or wake up the sleeping twins, she climbed the steps. Standing in the upstairs hall, she looked around once more. Her father was still on the porch. Her mother was downstairs working on a quilt. If she moved quickly, no one would know what she was doing.

Tina paused at the doorway to Charles's room. She couldn't help wondering whether Charles would have said yes to Sarah's request to drive a wagon with Tillie hidden in the back. He seemed fearless. He would have thought it was a great adventure to have a job in the Underground Railroad. He would not have thought twice about the risks involved—the danger to Tillie or the danger to himself. He would have jumped at the chance to do whatever Sarah asked.

Charles did not think enough before leaping into action. Tina was convinced of that. But maybe she thought too much. She worried about every little thing that might go wrong. Even taking some clothes for Tillie—she worried that Charles might catch her and be angry, or that Levi Coffin would not find the bundle in his store, or that what she chose would not be a good disguise for Tillie.

This is nonsense, Tina told herself harshly. *Just get in there and do what you have to do.*

She stepped into Charles's room. It was furnished much like her room: a single bed, a nightstand, a chest of drawers for his clothes. The chest had five drawers. Tina knew that two of the drawers had papers and railroad drawings in them. Charles did not spend a lot of time fretting over his clothes.

Carefully, she opened the first drawer. Four shirts greeted her. They were fairly new. Tina knew they all fit Charles very well.

The next drawer yielded two pairs of pants, one that he wore to school a lot, and the other that he wore to church.

The third drawer—the last one to offer any hope—proved to be what she needed. It held three shirts and a pair of pants. The knees of the brown pants had been patched more than once, until Mama had insisted that Charles stop wearing them. The sleeves of the shirts had become too short for his gangly arms.

A familiar creak told Tina that someone was coming up the stairs. The third step from the bottom always made that sound. Her father frequently said he was going to fix it, but he never did. Tina was glad he hadn't.

Quickly, Tina snatched up the pants and a blue cotton plaid shirt. She rolled them into a ball and tucked them under one arm before dashing out of the room. Just as she opened the door to her own room, she caught sight of Charles on the stairs in the corner of her eye. She avoided his glance.

Inside her room, she threw herself on her bed. After taking a moment to catch her breath, she pulled the clothes out from under her arm and held them up in front of her. They were on the ragged side, especially the pants, but she was sure they would successfully transform Tillie into a lazy-looking teenage boy. Tillie would appear to be the opposite of everything she truly was.

Tina rolled the clothes up again and stuffed them under her pillow. First thing in the morning, she would bundle them up. She would leave for school early and go out of her way to visit Levi Coffin's store. Once she had done this, once the bundle was someone else's responsibility, Tina would be able to breathe easier. Her life could go back to normal.

Tina squeezed her eyes shut and pressed her lips together. Silently she said a prayer for Tillie. Then she added another one for Hubert. She had never met Hubert, but still she hoped that some day Tillie and Hubert would find each other again.

The room had grown dark. Tina undressed and went to bed.

The next morning, Tina woke up while it was still dark. Immediately, her heart started racing. She had a lot to get done before school started, and she didn't want to raise anyone's suspicions.

Tina sat up on the edge of her bed and lit her candle. Then she hurriedly poured some water from a pitcher into her basin and washed her face. She slipped on her school dress, tied back her unruly red hair, and made her bed. Blowing out her candle, she quietly slipped downstairs so Charles wouldn't hear her and begin peppering her with questions about why she was already up and dressed.

"My, you're up early," Mama said as Tina entered the kitchen and helped herself to a bowl of oatmeal.

"I promised Sarah I would stop by the store for her on my way to school, so I wanted to leave myself plenty of time," Tina answered. While she wasn't telling Mama everything, Tina felt glad that she wasn't lying.

Before Mama could ask any more questions, noise from upstairs announced that the twins were awake.

"I guess I know where I'm needed," Mama said with a smile. "Your lunch is already packed in your lunch pail. Have a good day, dear." After dropping a quick kiss on Tina's forehead, Mama sailed upstairs to the now-screaming twins.

Tina gobbled the rest of her cereal and quickly washed

up her dishes. As she tiptoed up to her room, she could hear noise coming from Charles's room. If she hurried, she might make it out of the house before Charles went down to breakfast.

She shut her bedroom door and grabbed the bundle of clothing she'd made the night before. Cradling it in her right arm, she draped her shawl around her shoulders and down over the bundle so it wouldn't show. Next she placed her schoolbooks on her right arm to disguise the bump that the bundle made under her shawl. Satisfied that she'd done the best she could, Tina took a deep breath and hurried down the stairs to the kitchen.

As she grabbed her pail, Tina heard Charles bounding down the stairs. She cringed. How was she going to get out of the house without Charles guessing something was up?

She reached for the back door handle and managed to get the right side of her body behind the open door before Charles's voice rang out.

"Hey, Tina! Where are you going so early?"

Tina glanced back over her shoulder at her younger brother. She tried to look casual, but she could tell Charles was very suspicious. "I'm running an errand for Sarah," she said calmly. "Mama knows all about it. I'll see you later at school."

"But Tina," Charles yelled. "What's that—"

Tina closed the door on his question and forced herself to walk sedately down the street. Sooner than she had expected, she was in Levi Coffin's store. She breathed a sigh of relief when she noticed that the store was almost empty. She spent a few minutes pretending to compare bolts of fabric in one corner of the store.

Looking around to make sure no one was nearby, Tina rested her bundle on the counter, hoping that it would blend in with the fabric. Then she quietly slipped out of the store, relieved that no one called after her to let her know she had left something behind.

As she turned up the street toward school, her heart froze. Reflected in the store's window was the image of Kenyon LeClaire leaning against the building across the street. What was that slave catcher doing outside Levi Coffin's store?

Chapter 13
Lost!

Tina tried to walk slowly, but it took everything in her to keep from running to school, running away from that hateful Kenyon LeClaire. When she reached the corner and prepared to cross the street, she glanced back at Mr. LeClaire. He wasn't looking in her direction, nor had he moved. He seemed intent on watching the people who entered and left Mr. Coffin's store. Was he trying to identify those who might sympathize with escaped slaves?

Tina tried to think of other reasons for Mr. LeClaire to be watching Mr. Coffin's store. As a slave catcher, he wouldn't be buying something in a store supported by abolitionists.

And she knew he wasn't a Quaker because he'd gone to services in her own church that Sunday. No, Tina was convinced Mr. LeClaire was up to no good, and it worried her.

Although Tina forced herself to walk slowly, it was still early when she got to school. To her surprise, Sarah was already there. "Sarah!" Tina called to her friend.

The Quaker girl smiled and walked over to Tina. "Didst thou deliver the package?" she asked quietly.

"Yes," Tina answered. "But I think there may be a problem. As I was leaving the store, I noticed the slave catcher, Kenyon LeClaire, leaning up against the building across the street."

"Was he there when thou first arrived?" Sarah asked.

Tina thought hard for a moment. "No," she finally answered. "I'm sure he wasn't because I remember being so relieved that no one was on the street and hardly anyone was inside the store. I'm sure I would have noticed him if he'd been there."

"That is good," Sarah said, looking relieved. "He would not have had the opportunity to notice if thou wast carrying anything when thou entered the store, so he wouldn't notice that thou left a package behind. Thou shouldst be safe, but as a precaution, thou shouldst avoid that area for several weeks."

Sarah glanced around to make sure no one could hear their conversation. "We have been concerned about Mr. LeClaire's activities," she said in a hushed voice to Tina. "He seems to be trying to identify those of us who sympathize with the abolitionist cause and may be helping escaped slaves. That is one reason we are looking for different people to make deliveries."

"Deliveries of what?" a new voice asked.

Tina groaned inwardly. Trust Charles to be precisely where he wasn't wanted. Before she could respond, Sarah gave her a warning look.

"Good morning, Charles," Sarah said, smiling at Tina's younger brother. "I was discussing with thy sister the difficulty of getting messages and shopping lists to Mr. Coffin. As thou noticed weeks ago when thee and thy sister met me while shopping, his store is some distance from my home. Yet my mother wishes to support his endeavors. Thy sister's help is greatly appreciated by my mother."

Just then the bell rang. Tina smiled when she saw Charles's disappointed face. She knew he was full of questions, but they would have to remain unasked. Classes were about to begin.

"Let's go there!" Daria said. She pointed a chubby finger enthusiastically to a shop across the street.

"Yes, let's go there!" David pointed vaguely in the same direction.

Tina sighed. She could never be sure what the twins were pointing at. They were so excited about spending part of Saturday downtown with her. No matter what store they went in, the twins would find something to touch and explore.

"You heard what Mama said," Tina answered them. "We're to go to the general store and look at the yard goods. She needs some quilting quarters and thread to finish off the quilt."

In the basket hanging on her arm, Tina carried some samples of the fabrics that had already been worked into the quilt. Most of them came from old clothes and scraps from other projects that Mama had collected from everyone in the family. But she needed a few more pieces to finish the quilt. Rather than wait for someone to outgrow something green, she had decided to splurge and buy a swatch of fabric or two. She was not particular about the pattern, as long as it was green. So that afternoon, she had sent Tina out to do the errand. The twins had insisted on tagging along.

"Are we going to buy candy?" David asked.

"No, we're going to buy fabric. Just fabric."

"But we could buy candy, too," Daria said.

"Let's buy candy, too," David echoed.

"No, we're buying fabric. Green fabric. And some quilting thread. Mama's going to finish her quilt, and you'll both see how beautiful it is."

"But I don't want a quilt. I already have one. I want candy."

"Me, too!"

Tina adjusted her bonnet with her free hand and changed her grip on the basket. She tried to think what to say to quiet the twins.

"We want to obey Mama, don't we?" she said.

"Yes," Daria said emphatically. "Children, obey your parents. The Bible says that."

"That's right. Mama sent us to buy fabric swatches. So we'll obey her."

She took a few steps down the street. The twins followed.

"Tina?"

"Yes, Daria?"

"Does the Bible say it's wrong to buy candy?"

Tina sighed. "No, Daria. I don't think the Bible says anything about candy."

"Did Mama say it was wrong to buy candy?"

"No, not exactly." Mama had not said anything about candy, and Tina wished that she had. Then she could simply tell the twins that they couldn't buy candy.

"Then we won't be disobeying if we buy some."

Tina sighed again. How could she argue with this logic?

"Can we? Can we?" David started jumping up and down. "This shirt bothers me," he said. He stopped jumping and started fidgeting with the buttons. In a split second, he had three of them undone.

Tina instantly stooped in front of him. She buttoned his shirt. "David, we must keep our clothes on while we are downtown. It's not proper to walk around without clothes."

"But it bothers me."

"As soon as we get home, we'll find your favorite shirt, and you can change."

"That's a long time."

"Well, then, let's hurry to the general store."

"What about the sweet shop?" Daria asked. "That's where they have candy."

Tina let her shoulders sag. Why had she agreed to bring the twins on this errand? It would take her four times as long as it should just to buy a yard or two of fabric. And she would be exhausted by the time she got home.

She was already tired. She had been tired all week. Worrying all the time, Tina had discovered, was very tiring.

But she had worried all week, wondering if Tillie was safe. Had Sarah found someone to take Tillie to the meeting spot, or had her parents risked taking her themselves? Had the wagon been stopped and searched? Was Kenyon LeClaire still in town? Did he suspect that Tina was involved with the abolitionists? Was he on Tillie's trail? After following her for months, he was not likely to give up easily now.

Questions flooded Tina's mind constantly. But there were never any answers. Since she had told Sarah she could not help with Tillie's transportation, Tina knew no details. She did not even know what day the meeting was supposed to happen. During her trip to Levi Coffin's store, she had been careful to follow Sarah's instructions to the letter. Tina had not even spoken with either of the Coffins, although she'd met them several times over the years.

After her brief conversation with Sarah on Monday morning, she had heard nothing from her friend all week. Tillie could be safe in Canada by now—maybe even with Hubert. Or she could still be squeezed into that space in the wall behind the cabinet, fearfully waiting for someone to guide her to safety. Tina had no way of finding out.

She was not even sure if Sarah would want to see her again. Perhaps her reluctance to help with the activity of the Underground Railroad had cost her the friendship. A sob stuck in Tina's throat. She hated to think she might have lost her best friend because of her fearfulness.

And then there was the matter of Charles. He had been behaving unusually all week. Ever since that conversation in the schoolyard Monday morning, he hadn't asked a single question about Sarah and Tina's activities. But he did spend a lot of time staring at Tina. It was getting on her nerves.

Tina realized that David and Daria were not keeping up with her. She stopped and looked behind her. The twins straggled about ten feet apart from each other, both overwhelmed by the sights and sounds of downtown Cincinnati. On a Saturday afternoon, a lot of people were out shopping. The streets were busy, both with people walking and with carriages and wagons.

"Come on, you two," Tina said encouragingly. "We have to walk a little more quickly."

"Where is the sweet shop, Tina?" Daria asked. She stood with two fingers in her mouth, as she often did when she was puzzling over something.

"It's on the other side of the street, in the next block."

"Good. We haven't passed it yet." The fingers came out of her mouth and she skipped to catch up with Tina.

"Come on, David. Catch up!" Daria called.

David's little legs pumped a little harder. He took Daria's hand. They looked very cute together, Tina thought. Daria's hair was just a little more reddish than David's brown head, but they were about the same size and clearly attached to each other. Her heart softened. She was not so sorry she had agreed to bring them along.

Tina continued on down the street, trying to remember to pace herself to the twins. She could not possibly carry them both, so she had to slow down.

As she glanced across the street to scan the shops, a flash of blue plaid passed by Tina's eyes. Blue plaid cotton. Tina looked again, more carefully. Across the street, a black teenage boy with slumped shoulders and a scowl shuffled into a shop. He wore a gray cap, patched brown pants, and a blue plaid cotton shirt. Most of the time, his eyes watched the ground in front of him. He slid his feet along sloppily, slouching all the time.

Tina could not believe her eyes. The transformation was incredible. If she had not recognized the clothes, she was certain she would not have recognized Tillie. The figure she saw enter the shop looked nothing like the frightened but refined young woman she had met ten days earlier.

But what was Tillie doing walking around the streets of Cincinnati in broad daylight? Surely she knew that was dangerous. She had come all the way from Georgia, in the Deep South, traveling at night. Why would she now walk around in the daytime?

"I want red licorice."

"No, I want black licorice."

"Red!"

"Black!"

"Red!"

Tina looked down just in time to see David start to slap his twin. She caught him by the wrist.

"No, no, David. No fighting."

"But she won't let me buy any black licorice. She says we have to get red."

"Daria, please, why must you make David so angry?"

"He thinks black licorice is better than red, but he's wrong."

"David can choose whatever licorice he likes best."

"Does that mean we are going to buy some licorice?"

Trapped—by a four-year-old's logic!

"I didn't say that. Why don't we get the yardage first and see if we have any pennies left over?"

"We're going to buy candy! We're going to buy candy!" Daria was triumphant.

"But first let's get Mama's fabric."

How does she manage to do this to me? Tina wondered. In only one block, Daria had worn her down. Tina had gone from saying quite clearly that they were not going to buy any candy to promising to stop at the sweet shop after the general store.

Now the twins skipped ahead of her, eager to get the official errand done so they could cross the street to the sweet shop.

Tina glanced across the street, hoping to catch sight of the blue plaid shirt. Inwardly, she scolded herself for taking her eyes from the street to look at the twins. Now she had no idea where Tillie was.

Tina turned back to her own side of the street.

"Daria, David, wait for me!" They were getting too far ahead of her. She would have to catch up with them.

Reluctantly, Tina glanced over her shoulder one more time. She sucked in her breath abruptly. Coming down the street from the other direction, on the other side, was a tall, well-dressed man in a black suit, carrying a polished dark wood cane. He paused only long enough to look at his watch. Kenyon LeClaire was only three shops away from where Tina had last seen Tillie. Her eyes flew to the nearby shops, desperately looking for a patch of blue plaid.

A wagon rumbled down the street and stopped—right in front of Tina. The wagon was drawn by two large black horses and was loaded high with hay.

Tina could not see a thing on the other side of the street—not Kenyon LeClaire, not Tillie, not anything. She stood on her tiptoes to try to see over the horses. She bent sideways to try to look between the wagon and the hitch. She could not see a thing.

She glanced at the twins. Thankfully, they had stopped to look at the wagon and were not far off. Daria had her fingers in her mouth again, trying to think what to make of the large wagon and its load.

"You said the sweet shop was on the other side of the street," Daria said anxiously.

"Yes, it is," Tina said, with far less patience than she normally had with Daria.

"How will we get there if the wagon is in the way?"

"The wagon will move. Just be patient."

But Tina had no patience herself. The wagon driver had gotten down and gone into a shop. She had no idea how long the wagon would be parked there.

"We can go around the wagon," Tina said. "Follow me."

And she led the way past the wagon until she had a clear view of the other side of the street.

"I see the sweet shop!" Daria cried out with much relief.

"Yes, there it is," Tina said. She did not see what she was looking for. Neither Tillie nor Kenyon LeClaire were in sight.

Please, God, Tina prayed silently, *keep Tillie safe. Show me what to do.*

At last she saw the patch of blue plaid. She reminded herself that if she had not recognized the clothes, she would not have known it was Tillie walking through the shops. After all the months that Tillie had been away from Georgia, Kenyon LeClaire was not likely to recognize Tillie in her disguise. Still, Tina was nervous.

Tillie entered another shop. Kenyon LeClaire went into the shop two doors down. He was getting closer—too close. Tina had to do something right away. *With God's help, I will,* she thought.

Suddenly she felt that it was urgent that she cross the street. "Come on," Tina said to the twins. "I've changed my mind. Let's go to the sweet shop first."

She reached out a hand and felt one chubby, sticky hand take hers.

"Where's Daria?" David asked softly.

Tina spun around. Sure enough, Daria was nowhere in sight. Had she been there the last time Tina looked down? Tina could not remember.

"Did you see which way she went?" Tina asked David.

The little boy just shrugged. "Daria went away."

"We must find her," Tina said urgently. She looked across the street again. Again she felt the sense of urgency to cross the street. But she must find Daria first.

"Daria? Daria, answer me."

Tina held David's hand very firmly as she brushed past other people walking down the street. The little boy was almost swallowed up in one hoop skirt when Tina pressed against a woman too closely.

"Daria! Daria!"

Across the street, Tina saw a flash of blue plaid. Panic swelled in her heart.

"Daria! Daria!"

CHAPTER 14
The Rescue

David squirmed to get away from Tina.

"You're squeezing my hand!" he cried.

"I don't want to lose you, too," Tina said impatiently. But she loosened her grip slightly. She knew David was far less likely to run off than Daria was, and she did not mean to hurt him.

Tina started retracing her steps, going back to where she had stood behind the hay wagon. That was the last place she was certain she had seen Daria. She reacted to every swish of a skirt, every tap of a gentleman's cane, hoping that her little sister was the source of the sound. Daria was nowhere to be seen.

"Maybe she crossed the street," Tina said aloud. After all, the sweet shop was on the opposite side of the street, and Daria had her heart set on getting there.

"We're not allowed to cross the street," David declared.

"But Daria might have done it anyway."

However, the hay wagon was not the only obstacle in the street. Carriages went by every few minutes. People milled around in groups exchanging leisurely Saturday afternoon greetings. It did not seem possible to Tina that a small child like Daria would have been able to cross the street so fast. But then, Daria was always quicker than anyone expected.

Tina tried to control her panic. She finally decided it would be easier to carry David. She scooped him up and walked more rapidly up and down the street.

At one point, she forced herself to stand still and study the other side of the street. Daria might be over there, after all. Tillie and Kenyon LeClaire were certainly over there. She peered into the doorways from a distance and scanned the sidewalks. She did not see Daria or Tillie. But Kenyon LeClaire, with his distinctive height, was easy to spot. He stood outside a store checking his watch. Tina's heart leaped to her throat. She had to get across the street.

"Where's Daria?" David asked several times. His voice was becoming frightened.

Tina held him a little tighter. "We'll find her. Don't worry. She can't have gone far." She brought her attention back to her side of the street.

A poke in the back made Tina spin around.

"Looking for something?" Charles grinned at Tina. He

was holding Daria.

"Charles! Thank goodness you found her. I couldn't see her anywhere. I was afraid she had tried to cross the street."

"She did try," Charles said. "And she made it. I found her in front of the sweet shop on my way home from the railroad station."

"I found the lollipop store," Daria said proudly.

"I can't believe she got away from me and all the way across the street so fast." Even in her annoyance, Tina was glad to see her little sister safe.

Daria pouted now. "Charles wouldn't buy me any red licorice."

"I don't have any pennies," Charles said in his own defense.

Tina scowled at Daria. "You've been naughty. I don't know if you ought to have licorice now."

"But I want it," Daria wailed.

"Me, too!" David joined in.

"They're driving me crazy," Tina complained to Charles. "I can't make them stop nagging about getting candy."

"Speaking of candy," Charles said, "I saw something mighty strange across the street in front of the sweet shop."

"What was that?" Tina's eyes flashed to the other side of the street.

"Someone was wearing my shirt."

Tina kept her voice steady. "Why would someone be wearing your shirt? How is that possible?"

"That's what I wondered. A black boy was wearing it." His brown eyes bore into Tina's green eyes. "It was that blue plaid shirt that Mama made me. It wasn't a store-bought shirt. It was the one Mama made. That's why I know it was mine."

"Blue plaid?" Tina said. "I did the buttonholes on that shirt. I thought it didn't fit you anymore."

"It doesn't," Charles said. "But it's still my favorite."

"Someone else could have bought the same fabric. They sell it at the general store. That's where Mama got it."

"It was my shirt," Charles insisted. "Mama wanted to keep that shirt for David to wear some day. I know she wouldn't give it away."

Tina shrugged. "It's just an old shirt, Charles—one that you don't wear anymore anyway."

As uncomfortable as Tina was with Charles's questions, she was paying more attention to the activity across the street than she was to Charles. Tillie had been in the same shop for a long time now. Kenyon LeClaire was getting quite close. In only a few minutes, he would be in the same store with Tillie. Tina wished she knew whether LeClaire was just asking questions or whether he knew that Tillie was nearby. Either way, Tina knew she had to do something. As good as Tillie's disguise was, Tina did not want to see it tested by Kenyon LeClaire.

"Funny thing about that shirt," Charles said. "The last time I saw it in my drawer was last Saturday. Then Sunday you take a ride with Meg out toward Sarah's home. And Monday you make a delivery for her at Levi Coffin's store. Now was that a shopping list or a shirt you were delivering?" He looked at her with sudden understanding. "Has my timid sister suddenly become involved in the railroad business?"

"Charles," Tina said in frustration, "don't be ridiculous. I can't do anything about your shirt. It may be gone. Mama may have donated it during one of the clothing drives. But Mama sent me down here on an errand, and I don't want to go home empty-handed. I'm just tired of having the twins with me. I thought if you were going home, you could take them."

Charles groaned. "But you already said that they're whining and nagging. Why would I want to take them?"

"Would it hurt you so much to show some responsibility once in awhile?"

"What's that supposed to mean?"

Tina did not answer.

Charles followed Tina's gaze across the street. "Hey, that's Kenyon LeClaire," he said. "I heard at the station that he caught one of his slaves and that he thinks he knows where another one is."

"Which one?" Tina asked. Her eyes were fixed across the street.

Charles shrugged. "I don't know. The housemaid one, I think."

Tina did not respond. She clutched David so tightly that he started to protest.

"Don't squeeze me!" the boy howled.

Tina paid no attention. Tillie came out of a store and leaned against the outside of it. She seemed to be staring straight at Tina. But if she recognized Tina, she gave no sign of it. After a moment, she shuffled down the block and disappeared into another shop.

"Tina?" Charles asked softly.

She did not answer.

"Tina!" he repeated. "You saw him, didn't you—the boy with my shirt."

Tina smiled inwardly. Charles was still convinced the person who wore his shirt was a boy.

"Yes." She turned to look at Charles reluctantly. They each still held a squirming twin. They looked at each other for a long time, neither of them speaking. Tina's heart pounded so hard she was sure Charles could hear it.

Charles reached out and took David out of Tina's arms. "I'll take the twins home," he said. "I can see you may need to make a stop at the railroad station."

Once again, he looked into her eyes. As Tina met his gaze, understanding passed between them.

"Thank you, Charles," Tina said, incredibly surprised and grateful.

"I don't want to go home!" Daria protested. "I want licorice."

"I promise I'll get you a piece and bring it home to you," Tina said. "Just go with Charles now."

"You really promise?"

"I really promise."

"Really, truly promise?"

"Really, truly promise."

"I want red."

"I'll remember."

Finally, Daria stopped her protests. Charles set the twins down, took them by the hands, and led them toward home.

Tina scanned the street again, hoping she had not missed

anything. Kenyon LeClaire was standing outside the shop that Tillie was in, checking his watch. Tina was grateful for that silly habit of his. If he did not spend so much time checking the time, he might have caught up to Tillie by now.

Tina lifted her skirt with both hands and scrambled across the street. She did not have the slightest idea what she would do when she got there, but she knew she had to go.

Breathless, she came to a stop next to Kenyon LeClaire.

"Mr. LeClaire, how nice to see you on this fine day," Tina said loudly and brightly.

LeClaire gave her a strange look.

"I'm sorry, sir," she continued. "Of course, you don't know me. My name is Christina Fisk. I believe you've met my brother Charles at the railroad station. He has mentioned you to me on several occasions."

LeClaire was a bit flustered, but still polite. "Of course, I remember. Charles, yes, I remember."

"He's quite eager to know everything about the railroad."

"As I recall, he is not overly eager for work, even if he would be well paid."

"That's my brother," Tina declared. "We all think that he ought to learn some responsibility. Why, you should hear the way my mother has to nag him about his schoolwork."

"It's been very nice meeting you, Miss Fisk," Kenyon LeClaire said. "If you'll excuse—"

Tina moved slightly to block his path.

"I understand you are a regular visitor to Cincinnati. Charles says that this is not your first visit."

"Yes, I have been here several times. It is a lovely city."

"What brings you to Cincinnati?"

He paused for a moment before saying, "My work." He tipped his hat. "Good afternoon, Miss Fisk."

Tina persisted. "Charles pointed you out to me in church last Sunday. We were both so encouraged to see you visiting our church. I do hope you enjoyed the service."

"Yes, it was quite nice." He was looking over her head.

"Is it very like your church at home?"

"Quite similar, yes." He took a step forward. Tina moved right along with him, stepping backward.

"And where are you from? I don't believe Charles mentioned that to me."

"I'm from Northern Georgia," he said with a drawl.

"You've come such a long way from home," Tina said, her heart pounding. "You must miss your family. Do you have any family in this area?"

"Thank you for your kind inquiry," he said politely. "I regret that I have no relatives in the North. I hope to be going home to my family quite soon."

Tina casually turned around so she was facing the same direction as Mr. LeClaire. She wanted to see what he was seeing. He looked toward the shop that Tillie was in. Tina caught sight of the familiar blue. She was glad she had chosen that bright shirt rather than one of the dull ones that had been in the drawer with it. Tillie was just inside the doorway of the shop, probably coming out soon.

Tina leaned to one side, just enough to lose her balance. The contents of her basket spilled to the sidewalk. Fabric, thread, pins, and coins scattered in every direction.

"How clumsy of me," she said. When she stooped to pick up the fabric swatches and thread, Tina placed herself squarely between Kenyon LeClaire and the shop door. She could see her face in his polished black boots.

She spoke quite loudly, partly because she was more nervous than she had ever been in her whole life and partly because she wanted Tillie to hear her.

"My mother is working on a quilt. She sent me on a simple errand, and so far I have managed to lose my little sister and spill my basket. I can't imagine what I will do next."

Kenyon LeClaire hesitated ever so slightly. Then he did what Tina had calculated a Southern gentlemen would feel obligated to do. He stooped to help her pick up her scattered items.

"It's quite a beautiful quilt," Tina said, as she picked up scraps of fabric. "It has a lovely pattern all done in shades of green. But, of course, you can see that in these scraps."

"I'm sure that your mother does exquisite work." Mr. LeClaire started to stand up.

With her left foot, Tina managed to kick a spool of thread so that it rolled away from the shop.

"Thank you ever so much for your help, Mr. LeClaire," Tina said. "Would you mind?" She gestured toward the rolling thread.

Kenyon LeClaire moved to the side, chasing the thread. He was anxious to do his gentlemanly duty quickly and be on his way. While he was turned away, Tillie darted out of the shop, around a corner, and down an alley.

"I am ever so embarrassed," Tina said, standing up and

brushing her hair out of her eyes. Kenyon LeClaire handed her the stray thread. "I certainly did not intend to disturb your afternoon. I only meant to say hello and to welcome you to our city. You must think me a silly child."

Tina did not care what Kenyon LeClaire thought of her, as long as Tillie got away.

"Not at all," he said, "you are a most delightful young woman. I am enchanted to meet you." He bowed slightly toward her, his great height towering over her small frame. "And now, if you'll excuse me, I have a pressing business engagement."

"Certainly, Mr. LeClaire. Good day. I hope you enjoy the remainder of your stay."

Once again he tipped his hat. Then he turned and walked away.

Tina emptied her lungs in one long breath. She could not believe what she had just done. But Tillie had gotten away. That was what mattered most.

CHAPTER 15

Tina Takes a Stand

For a while that Saturday afternoon, Tina wondered if her body ever would return to normal. She felt her knees knocking as she stopped at the sweet shop to buy the red and black licorice. Her legs continued to shake as she crossed the street to the general store and looked at the bolts of green fabric. Then when she paid for her purchases, her hand was shaking so badly that the clerk looked up at her face with concern.

"Are you all right, miss?" he asked politely. "Perhaps you'd like to sit here awhile and drink some water. It's mighty warm out there, and I'd hate to think of you having a spell on your way home."

Embarrassed as she was by all the attention, Tina thought it might not be a bad idea to sit for a few minutes and give her heart a chance to stop racing. By the time she finished drinking the water the clerk had brought to her, she was breathing evenly and deeply. She did not think anyone else would suspect something was bothering her. But she was more tired than she'd ever imagined a person could be.

It took longer than usual for Tina to walk home. No one was on the porch that afternoon as she trudged up the street. Tina wearily climbed the steps and dropped into a wooden rocker her Uncle Ben had made years ago. She gave a little push with her toes and let the motion soothe her. The chair squeaked every time it moved backward. Tina hardly noticed.

Tina was bone tired, but peaceful. She felt sure she would sleep soundly that night, deeply satisfied with what she had done that afternoon. A simple Saturday errand had turned into the most important day in her life. She would never be able to walk down that street in downtown Cincinnati without reliving what had happened that day. She remembered every moment, from the first time she'd sighted Tillie until she'd watched Kenyon LeClaire walk away. It was all permanently burned into her brain.

But most of all, Tina remembered every feeling of the afternoon, every beat of her heart, every lost breath. Tina had done what needed to be done. "With God's help," she said quietly to herself.

The front door squeaked open and Daria and David thundered out onto the porch. Their mother was right behind.

"Tina's home!" Daria announced. "I want my licorice now."

"Did you get black?" David asked.

Tina stopped rocking, reached down for her basket, and sat up straight. "Black is what you wanted, so black is what you got!" she said. And she produced the black licorice.

David squealed his delight.

"But I wanted red!" Daria groaned.

"Red is what you wanted, so red is what you got!" And Tina pulled out the red licorice.

Daria took her candy and skipped to the other end of the porch.

"Here, Mama," Tina said, offering the basket to her mother. "I think you'll like what I found. Mr. Peterson said they were new."

Pamela Fisk took the basket from her tired daughter and peeked inside. Four squares of green calico in different patterns, as well as a spool of white quilting thread met her eyes. "These will be perfect. You have such good taste."

"Thank you, Mama."

"Imagine my surprise when Charles turned up at home with the twins," Mama said, settling into a chair next to Tina. "You have so much more patience with them than he does. I suppose they must have been quite a handful today.

Otherwise, you would not have sent them home with Charles."

Tina nodded. "I thought maybe I could finish the shopping more quickly without them. They are not really interested in looking at calico prints."

"No, I suppose not." Mama fingered the new fabric. "What surprised me even more is that Charles came home and went straight to the kitchen to do his homework. It's only Saturday afternoon, and I haven't reminded him about it even once."

Tina smiled. "That is certainly unusual." But then Charles had done several unusual things lately.

"I suppose the shops were as busy as they always are on Saturday afternoons," Mama remarked. "So many people go downtown on Saturdays just to walk around with no real purpose."

Tina nodded. "Yes, there were a lot of people."

For the first time, it occurred to her that a lot of people might have been watching her escapade with Kenyon LeClaire. She had been very brash in approaching a strange man and speaking to him as she did. She had spoken loudly enough for Tillie to hear her, so half of Cincinnati probably had heard her silly chatter as well. And then spilling her basket and making LeClaire crawl around on the sidewalk chasing a spool of thread—she had made quite a spectacle of herself. Sooner or later a report would reach her mother, and Tina would have some explaining to do. But not this afternoon. For now, she did not want to tell anyone what had happened. Since she could not tell the whole story, it was better not to say anything at all.

Tina was glad she had seen Tillie again. Rather than remembering her as frail and frightened, her last vision of Tillie was that of a healthy young woman with the energy to run from her pursuer. She would never see Tillie again. Tina knew that. She would never know what had brought Tillie out in broad daylight or why she had been going from shop to shop. But none of that mattered. She was just glad Tillie was safe from Kenyon LeClaire. Perhaps tonight, traveling by moonlight, Tillie would begin her journey to Canada, following the North Star once again.

Tina stood up and said to her mother, "I have to see Charles doing his homework with my own eyes."

Mama chuckled. "You'd better see it now. It may not last long."

Tina went into the house, through the dining room, to the kitchen. When the door had swung closed behind her, she said softly, "Hello, Charles."

"Hello, Tina." Charles did not even lift his head from his book.

"Charles," Tina began, "this afternoon—"

"Glad I was there to help," Charles said, before she even finished her sentence. He looked up at her. His strong brown eyes stared at her without blinking.

"I'm glad you were there, too," Tina said.

Charles bent over his book again. "I have to finish this. I have a lot to catch up on if I'm going to be a lawyer some day."

"A lawyer?" Tina said, surprised. "I thought you wanted to drive a train."

"Even the railroad needs lawyers," Charles said. "After

all, Uncle Tim does both." He lifted his eyes and looked at her.

Tina understood. Charles was not talking about the trains he loved to visit at the station.

"I'll leave you alone, then," Tina said, and turned to leave.

"Just remember," Charles said, "you owe me a shirt."

Tina smiled. "I'll remember. I know just the fabric."

She went upstairs to the silence and solitude of her bedroom. As soon as the door was closed, Tina reached under the mattress and pulled out her secret copy of *Uncle Tom's Cabin.* She settled herself comfortably on her bed, sitting cross-legged, and began to read. "The hunt was long, animated, and thorough, but unsuccessful."

That's right, Mr. Kenyon LeClaire, Tina thought. *The hunt is long and unsuccessful. You will never find Tillie.*

Tina had been reading steadily through the book all week. Now she was almost done. Her only regret was that she had not read the book sooner. She was going to tell Uncle Tim that she had it. In fact, she was going to tell everyone she had read *Uncle Tom's Cabin,* and she was going to be proud of it. She wondered if Sarah had read it.

Sarah. Tina wished she had had the courage to say yes to Sarah a week ago. What a difference seven days could make. But it was not the week that had changed her. It was the experiences of one afternoon, one ordinary Saturday afternoon, and a piece of blue plaid cloth.

Tina knew she would never speak of today with Sarah. She would never ask Sarah what had become of Tillie. But if she ever stumbled upon another "guest" of the Henrys',

Tina would be ready to do what needed to be done.

"With God's help," she said aloud to an empty room.

"Tina?" Daria was jiggling the doorknob, trying to get in. "Mama says you are to come to supper now."

"I'll be right there," Tina said. Once again she had not realized how long she had read. Evening had come.

Tina marked her place in the book and closed it. Out of habit, she started to push it back under her mattress. But she caught herself. Instead she laid the book on her nightstand, in plain view.

If reading *Uncle Tom's Cabin* meant that she was an abolitionist, then so be it. Christina Fisk had no regrets.

There's More!

The American Adventure continues with *Time for Battle.* When David and Daria Fisk meet TJ and DJ Baxter, they're glad to meet another set of twins. The boys have just moved to Cincinnati from South Carolina.

But the twins are even more excited about the idea of forming a baseball team. David is an excellent striker, TJ hurls better than anyone his age, and Daria and DJ are good fielders. With their friends, they form one of the best teams in town.

Unfortunately, Mrs. Baxter is not happy with her sons' Yankee friends and their ideas about slavery. And David and TJ begin fighting over the best way to run the team. Daria and DJ try to bring peace between their brothers, but nothing seems to work. Then war breaks out between the North and the South. Can anything save the twins' friendship now?